Nick wa...
almost kissed.

Technically it wasn't her first time, but Nick was a man. Somehow she knew he would have done the deed with confidence, finesse and thoroughness. He'd made her pulse pound, her heart race, and stolen the breath from her lungs without even touching his mouth to hers. Oh, how she wished he had!

If she wasn't careful, he would see that. What if he took her up on the invitation? She would be out of the frying pan into the fire.

How could she keep him from seeing how very much she wanted to feel his lips pressed against hers?

Dear Reader,

Compelling, emotionally charged stories featuring honorable heroes, strong heroines and the deeply rooted conflicts they must overcome to arrive at a happily-ever-after are what make a Silhouette Romance novel come alive. Look no further than this month's offerings for stories to sweep you away....

In *Johnny's Pregnant Bride,* the engaging continuation of Carolyn Zane's THE BRUBAKER BRIDES, an about-to-be-married cattle rancher honorably claims another woman—and another man's baby—as his own. This month's VIRGIN BRIDES title by Martha Shields shows that when *The Princess and the Cowboy* agree to a marriage of convenience, neither suspects the other's real identity...or how difficult *not* falling in love will be! In *Truly, Madly, Deeply,* Elizabeth August delivers a powerful transformation tale, in which a vulnerable woman finds her inner strength and outward beauty through the love of a tough-yet-tender single dad and his passel of kids.

And Then He Kissed Me by Teresa Southwick shows the romantic aftermath of a surprising kiss between best friends who'd been determined to stay that way. A runaway bride at a crossroads finds that *Weddings Do Come True* when the right man comes along in this uplifting novel by Cara Colter. And rounding out the month is Karen Rose Smith with a charming story whose title says it all: *Wishes, Waltzes and a Storybook Wedding.*

Enjoy this month's titles—and keep coming back to Romance, a series guaranteed to touch *every* woman's heart.

Mary-Theresa Hussey

Mary-Theresa Hussey
Senior Editor

Please address questions and book requests to:
Silhouette Reader Service
U.S.: 3010 Walden Ave., P.O. Box 1325, Buffalo, NY 14269
Canadian: P.O. Box 609, Fort Erie, Ont. L2A 5X3

AND THEN HE KISSED ME

Teresa Southwick

Silhouette

ROMANCE™

Published by Silhouette Books

America's Publisher of Contemporary Romance

To Karen Taylor Richman, for your unwavering support
and steady guidance. My profound gratitude.

And Joan Marlow Golan, for understanding my vision
and giving me the opportunity to write this book.
My sincere thanks.

 SILHOUETTE BOOKS

ISBN 0-373-19405-6

AND THEN HE KISSED ME

Copyright © 1999 by Teresa Ann Southwick

Visit us at www.romance.net

Printed in U.S.A.

TERESA SOUTHWICK

is a native Californian with ties to each coast, since she was conceived in the East and born in the West. Living with her husband of twenty-five years and two handsome sons, she is surrounded by heroes. Reading has been her passion since she was a girl. She couldn't be more delighted that her dream of writing full-time has come true. Her favorite things include: holding a baby, the fragrance of jasmine, walks on the beach, the patter of rain on the roof and, above all—happy endings.

Teresa also writes historical romance novels under the same name.

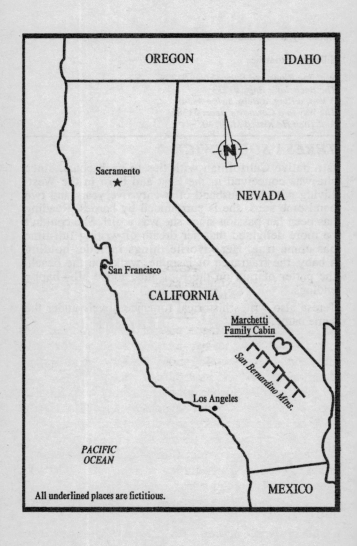

All underlined places are fictitious.

Chapter One

"**N**o kissing, Nick."

Abigail Ridgeway hurried past the wall of TV screens, all displaying the same Sunday football game.

"C'mon, Ab. What harm can a little kiss do?"

She stopped abruptly and turned. Six feet, two inches of Nick Marchetti made contact with some red-light parts of her five-foot-two-inch frame. He was her boss first, her friend second, and a hunk and a half she'd long ago placed a distant third.

She put a safe space between them now and looked up, way up. "This is not negotiable," she said. "There will be no hanky-panky, and that's final."

"Your expectations are unrealistic."

"Maybe. But you talked me into having this sweet-sixteen birthday party for my sister. I should at least get to set the ground rules," she said.

"Okay. But I'm warning you. A guy always wants what he can't have."

She grinned at him. "Is that personal experience

talking? The man who has everything? When did any-one ever tell you no?''

Abby hadn't thought his eyes could get any blacker, but they did. Intensity vibrated through him as he ran a hand through his short dark hair. His nose was straight, well-formed, and the wonderful masculine an-gles and planes of his face seemed to harden for a moment. She wondered what button she'd innocently put her finger on and how she could push it again. That was a wicked thought, and she made a mental note to work on her contrary streak.

But around Nick she sometimes couldn't help it. He was always so self-possessed that it was hard not to cheer when she discovered a chink in his armor. He had everything: beauty, brains, body, booty—as in more money than he knew what to do with. Anything that brought him down to the level of peons like herself seemed fair.

"This isn't about me, Abby. It's about Sarah. A girl only turns sweet sixteen once. It's a milestone. There should be some fanfare," he said, neatly circumventing her question. "Even though she asked me to convince you to let her have a party, I know you want it to be a success."

He'd turned the conversation back to her. In the five years she'd known him, she'd learned he was good at that. He had elevated the sidestep to an art form. "Okay. But Sarah is my responsibility. I'm her guard-ian. If my parents were still alive, maybe they would go along with your theory that a spirited game of spin the bottle is practically carved in stone at a teenage party. I disagree."

"Maybe you're right to be cautious. It's a well-known fact that sixteen-year-old, hormone-crazed boys

have the hots for older women." He tapped her nose.
"That would be you."

She frowned up at him. "Is this some new management technique? Did you learn this at that seminar?
Fractured reverse psychology?"

"You're not buying it?"

Shaking her head, she said, "Call me crazy, but I
think kissing games among teenagers that I'll be responsible for is asking for trouble. Just a guess, instinct
really. But that's all I've got."

"You've got me, pal," he answered, slipping his
hands into the pockets of his suit slacks. His sinfully
expensive matching jacket parted with the movement,
revealing a costly, crisp white shirt that hinted at the
washboard stomach beneath it.

"Right," she said, forcing her wayward thoughts in
a different direction. "You're awfully dressed up for
late Sunday afternoon. I thought you were supposed to
be off. Are you working today? Or do you have a
date?"

"Both," he said.

Nick Marchetti was a notorious workaholic. She
glanced sideways at her reflection in the blank big-
screen TV next to her that doubled for a mirror.
Smoothing her own rumpled suit skirt, she was
abruptly reminded that *she* was on a break from work.
Nick wasn't the boss that she reported to on a daily
basis. He was her *boss,* as in president of Marchetti's
Inc., big kahuna of the whole corporation.

She brushed a strand of her short blond bob back
into place, fluffed her straight bangs, then turned and
met Nick's gaze. "I didn't realize you had plans for
the evening or that you were working. Was there some-

thing specific you needed when you stopped in to the restaurant?''

He hesitated only a moment before answering with a shake of his head. "Just the usual."

She nodded. "Lucky for me you were free to help with my shopping. Although I have to get back to the restaurant soon. Can we table the party-games discussion to another time? Right now I need the expertise you so generously offered. This electronic stuff is confusing. I don't know a woofer from a hooter."

"I think you mean tweeter," he said, his mouth twitching as he tried not to laugh.

"See? What I know about these little black boxes with their digital readouts would fit on the head of a pin."

"Well I certainly feel cheap, degraded and disposable." His voice dripped with hurt feelings. He was such a faker.

She put her hand on her hip. "What are you talking about?"

"You want my expertise on electronic stuff, but not teenagers." He heaved an exaggerated sigh. "I feel so used."

She wanted to laugh, slug him gently in the arm and tell him to stuff a sock in it. But she was afraid that would be too forward. Nick made it easy to fall into friendly and familiar behavior. But Abby had an unbreakable law: always remember your position. Translation: never under any circumstances overstep your boundaries. There was only one problem—she was never quite sure where the line was. Maybe because of their shared history.

She had Nick to thank for her very first waitressing job. When she was eighteen, her parents had died in an automobile accident. Sarah had been eleven then. With no relatives to help, Abby had suddenly and shockingly become responsible for herself, as well as mother and father to her little sister. Although a total stranger, Nick gave her a job when no one else would. She'd walked into the restaurant he was managing at the time and asked for work. Abby had vowed to be his best employee ever, and so far she'd done well. She had worked her way through the ranks to assistant-manager-in-training of the local Marchetti's. She never let herself forget her promise to do him proud.

At all times, she tried to maintain a professional demeanor around him. But then he would say or do something outrageous, and she would forget that he was her boss. The buck stopped with him. He signed her paycheck. Actually his brother Luke did, but it was almost the same thing. It was okay for him to think of them as friends, but she knew better.

"The party is a month away," she said, instead of the teasing words on the tip of her tongue. "We have plenty of time to debate the issue of spin the bottle. But this sale is over today. I promised Sarah a CD player for her birthday. Good, bad or indifferent, I need to make a decision. Are you going to help me or—" she glanced at the milling salesmen "—let the circling sharks move in for the kill?"

He took her elbow and spun her toward the far wall filled with disc players and speakers. "You'd best thank your lucky stars that chivalry is alive and well." When she didn't say anything, he looked down at her and said, "What? No pithy comeback?"

She shook her head. "When you're right, you're right. I appreciate your help. If you'd told me you had a dinner date when you dropped in to the restaurant, I wouldn't have imposed.''

"You're not imposing."

"You're sure I'm not keeping you?"

"Nope. I've got plenty of time."

She looked at the display of equipment. "Should I go cheap, expensive or middle of the road? Should I sacrifice quality for features? Or get top-notch basic for the least amount of money?"

Nick pointed to a unit. "This is a good brand. It has all the features Sarah could possibly want. Unless she's missing the same electronic gene that you are. I think the cost is reasonable."

Abby's eyes widened as she looked at the price tag. "Maybe it's reasonable for a Marchetti. But it's way out of the Ridgeway budget—even at forty percent off."

"I could—"

"That's very nice of you, Nick. But I can't allow you to do it."

"You didn't let me finish."

"Excuse me, I shouldn't have interrupted. Speak your piece, *then* I'll refuse your offer to buy it for Sarah."

"I was going to suggest that you let me chip in. I don't know what to get her. You would be doing me a favor."

Abby knew this was one of his charitable gestures. He always found a way to make it seem as if it wasn't, but she had his number. His gift for creative maneuvering was probably the reason he'd taken Marchetti's from a successful restaurant to the fastest-growing chain in the Southwest. She wasn't sure why his benevolence suddenly rankled. Maybe because she was this close to finishing her degree, and would soon—finally—feel more independent. She didn't need his help. Along with her wicked streak, she would have to work on this inclination toward ingratitude that had only lately reared its ugly head.

Nick had been there for her when she had desperately needed someone. She had always tried to take care of things by herself, but he had never refused a request for help. Why did she now feel the need to do things on her own?

"I'll get the less expensive one," she said, pointing to another model by the same manufacturer. "It's a big-sister thing. I want to buy this for Sarah."

"What am I going to get her? I don't know much about sixteen-year-old girls."

"You knew she was dying to have a party."

"Kids love parties. That's not gender-specific. Besides, she told me. But the pressure of finding the right gift for a girl—"

"I'm sure Madison would be happy to help you pick something appropriate." Madison. A sophisticated name for a classy woman who was also beautiful, unusual—and Nick's girlfriend.

Abby had often seen them together. In addition to work-related functions, he frequently took her to dinner at the restaurant where Abby worked. He said he could always count on her to make sure the service and food were flawless. Abby figured he was showing off the beautiful, brilliant, back-East-educated Madison. She couldn't remember any woman in his life lasting as long as Ms. Wainright.

He had a funny look on his face. "Why don't you like her? Madison's a class act."

When had he learned to read her mind, Abby won-

dered? It wasn't that she disliked the other woman. Just
that Madison left her feeling woefully inadequate.
Madison was everything that Abby wasn't. She bent
over a pile of boxes to check model numbers, in order
to pick out the disc player she'd chosen. "I didn't say
I disliked Madison."

"No, but your tone spoke volumes about your feelings. Would you care to put them into words?"

"It's not my place to say anything."

"Is it safe to say that you believe she's not my
type?"

"Yes."

"Which means I'm *not* a class act?" He raised one
black eyebrow, but humor sparkled in his gaze.

"You're putting words in my mouth."

"In the six months Madison and I have dated, she's
been nothing less than charming, beautiful, smart and
successful. She would be an asset to any man."

She would certainly be his equal: beauty, brains,
body, booty. But he was right. For some reason Abby
couldn't put her finger on, she did think Madison
Wainright was wrong for him.

Abby often wondered how a great guy like Nick
Marchetti, who was good-looking enough to tempt a
card-carrying spinster, had managed to stay single.
Since he'd introduced the subject, she brought up a
question she just couldn't hold back.

"So why haven't you asked Madison to marry
you?"

"Is there a rule somewhere that says if a man ad-
mires positive attributes in a woman, he has to propose
to her?"

"Whoa. Just a little defensive, aren't we?"

"Nope. Not me." He looked sheepish. "Maybe. But

only because my mother and sister have been on my case.''

''Ever since Rosie got married and had her baby, you've softened on the settling-down issue. I get the impression that you're thinking about it.''

''It's crossed my mind.''

''So when are you going to ask Madison?''

He leaned a shoulder against the display rack and folded his arms across his chest. ''When are *you* going to settle down?''

''I've been settled down since I was eighteen. I'm heading toward footloose and fancy-free. In slightly less than two years, Sarah will graduate from high school and go to college. I see the light at the end of the tunnel.''

''You're still not dating, are you?''

Abby wondered how he could know that, when she was so careful to keep her personal and business lives separate. If he hadn't shown up at the restaurant and insisted, she wouldn't be shopping with him now. How could he know she didn't go out?

Then it hit her. Sarah didn't work for him and had no compunction about calling him up at the drop of a fingernail. She bent his ear with anything and everything that popped into her head. As far as Abby knew, he didn't mind. She figured if he did, any man who stood at the helm of a growing corporation could certainly clear the decks of one teenage girl if he wanted to. And Sarah was a talker. If talking was an Olympic event, her sister would take the gold.

''It's not like I can wiggle my nose and a man appears in a puff of smoke,'' Abby said. Now who was getting defensive, she thought, hearing that note in her voice.

"You can't tell me that men don't show an interest in an attractive woman like you."

She tried not to glow at his compliment, but was only partially successful. "I haven't noticed."

"Okay. I get the picture. You still shut them down cold. Let me give you a tip, pal. Guys need a little encouragement."

"Look, Nick," Abby said. She took a deep breath, trying to tamp down her irritation. If he had been just her friend, she would have given him an earful. But he was her boss, and she was struggling for a politically correct response. "Between work and school and raising Sarah, I don't have time right now. Once she's in college, it will be my turn. I'll have my degree in business. Right after I do footloose and fancy-free, next on my list is settling down."

Wait a minute. She had brought up the settling down subject—about *him*. Why was she suddenly defending herself? Oh, he was smooth. She'd hardly noticed him put her on the hot seat. Darn, he was good at shifting his backside out of the frying pan and putting hers in it.

"All work and no play," he said seriously.

"Okay, so Abby's a dull girl." She was teetering on the edge of the line she'd drawn, uncomfortable discussing herself with him. Two could play at turning the tables. "Are you going to bring Madison to Sarah's party?"

"Is she invited? I'm not even sure you want *me*. I *was* an afterthought."

"Nick, I've already explained that I didn't ask you to help me with the party because you're too busy."

"Is that all?" He frowned slightly.

"What else? Except that if I could afford the Green

Bay Packers defensive line, we wouldn't be having this conversation.''

"So I'm a poor substitute for your first choice?"

"No. But you work cheap. What about Madison? Would you like to bring her?"

"You almost sound sincere about wanting her there."

"It would be interesting to watch her play spin the bottle with a bunch of sixteen-year-old boys sporting sweaty palms and zits."

"Chaperones don't have to play. They referee." He looked at her, then raised one eyebrow. "You like her, don't you?"

"Yes," Abby answered honestly. She wasn't sure how he'd figured that out, but he was right. She admired and respected Madison very much. Which made the fact that she didn't think Madison Wainright was the woman for him even more puzzling.

"So Madison is invited?" he asked.

"She doesn't have to be invited. You're allowed to bring a date."

"I will, if you will." he said.

"Don't hold your breath," she muttered.

A few hours after their shopping trip, Nick stood in front of Abby's door. He had finished up his work early and didn't want to go home and kill time waiting for his date. He wasn't due to pick Madison up for an hour so he'd decided to stop at Abby's.

He wasn't sure why. Maybe because he hadn't been able to get her out of his mind. Partly because of work issues he hadn't discussed with her. But mostly her remark about not bringing a date to her sister's party. A pretty girl like Abby should have guys beating a path to her door, but he was the only one there. And the sidewalk didn't look any the worse for wear.

Her apartment was situated in a large complex with lots of shrubs and walkways. The entrance was tucked away between the stairway to the upper level and her storage unit.

He remembered helping her find the place after he'd advised her to sell her parents' home. It seemed best. She couldn't swing a mortgage payment, and she wouldn't take money from him. The proceeds went into trust for the two sisters. Abby had a lot of responsibility to shoulder and selling gave her freedom from the up-keep and burden of a house, as well as a bit of financial security.

That was good. Because the one thing he'd learned to count on from Abby was pride. No handouts. She wanted to do things on her own, and she had.

He pushed the button to ring the bell, and moments later Abby opened the door. Surprise at seeing him made her big blue eyes bigger and bluer.

"Nick. I thought you were having dinner with Madison."

"I am. In about an hour."

"This is a long way from her high-rent district. What are you doing here?"

"Just killing time," he said, unable to come up with anything he could share. "Do you mind if I come in?"

"Of course not. Sorry." She stepped back so that he could enter.

He surveyed the living room as she closed the door behind him. It wasn't large, but definitely homey and comfortable. A green-and-beige plaid couch and matching love seat sat at right angles to each other in the center. On one wall was an entertainment center with stereo, et cetera. He'd hooked it all up for her during an electronic crisis. It was one of the few times she'd called him. She didn't know what to plug in where and was afraid she'd blow up her new VCR or old TV. There was a small dining area adjacent to the tiny kitchen. He knew the rest of the place consisted of two bedrooms and baths, plus a laundry area with apartment-size appliances.

The walls were filled with collages of family photos, knickknacks and inexpensive prints. Prominently displayed was a bronze-colored metal plaque proclaiming, What Doesn't Kill Me Will Make Me Stronger.

"Can I get you something to drink?" Abby asked.

He shook his head. "Is Sarah here?"

"No. She went to the movies with a group of friends."

"Any of them guys?" he asked.

"If they were I'd be clothed in camouflage and doing surveillance. I wouldn't be standing here dressed like this," she said with an expansive hand gesture that indicated her work attire.

She was wearing the same suit he'd seen her in earlier, but it was a more casual, sexier look. The jacket was off, as were her high heels. There she stood in her stocking feet, a run creeping its way up from her shapely ankle. Her powder-blue silk blouse looked disheveled, half in, half out of the waistband of her navy skirt. Tousled straight blond hair surrounded her oval face. She looked as if she'd just engaged in a heavy necking session with a guy who had rounded first and was fast approaching second base.

The image took him completely by surprise. He'd never thought of her like that before. What surprised him more was his own reaction to the idea of her being with a man.

Irritation bordering on anger.

Correction, he thought. He wasn't angry at the idea of a man in her life, just the concept of that man actually reaching second base with her.

Since the day he'd met her, when she'd been eighteen trying to act thirty, he'd felt responsible for Abby. He'd taken the Ridgeway sisters under his wing. He'd given Abby her first job and watched her grow up. It was natural that he would want to protect her. But this level of intensity was weird, and he could only chalk it up to his encouraging her to date. Which he still thought she should do. It just meant that he would have to run interference for her.

She glanced at the watch on her slim wrist. "Isn't it kind of late for a dinner date?"

He took off his suit jacket and laid it on the arm of the love seat before sitting down. "Madison is preparing for a big court case this week. She needed more time. You're still filling in for Rebecca, aren't you?" he asked.

Abby nodded. "She's still on maternity leave. And I have to confess that wearing the manager's high heels is a real eye-opener."

"How so?" he asked. Although he already knew why. It was the reason he'd stopped into the restaurant earlier. But before he brought the subject up, he wanted to hear what she had to say. "You're home a little early, aren't you?"

She nodded, then tucked a strand of blonde hair behind her ear. "The dinner rush, if you can call it that, ended early, so I left."

He could tell by the shadows in her eyes, the slump

of her shoulders, the tension around her mouth that she was upset. "Tell me about it."

Sighing, she sat on the other sofa, far enough away that there was no danger of their knees brushing. Instead of turning toward him, she faced straight ahead. Her body language screamed *don't cross that line*. He frowned. At work she'd always made it a point to maintain a proper professional distance. Although lately he got the feeling she was trying to widen it. But this was her home. Here he thought they were friends, not boss and employee. Which was why he was letting her explain at her leisure the reason she was home earlier than usual.

"Business was slow. I had to send home a waiter and busboy tonight." She met his gaze. "That's the reason you were working today, isn't it? It's the reason you stopped in. You were checking things out."

"Yes." He didn't bother to deny it. He'd been afraid that a slow evening was what had sent her home early. "But I can see you're upset about sending employees home."

"Of course I am. It's not that I'm unclear on the concept."

"I never said you were."

"I know basic business principles. If the staffing ratio doesn't match income, the profit margin shrinks."

"That's true."

"Staff to a pattern."

"Right."

"The two newest employees are the first to go home early, and they're the ones who usually need the money the most."

"I understand."

"Jack, the waiter, has a wife and baby. Larry is

working his way through school.'' Tensely, she twisted
her fingers together.

Rank has its privileges, Nick thought. Low man on
the totem pole was the most vulnerable. But all the
logic in the world didn't make it any easier to stomach
telling an employee supporting a family that he wasn't
going to earn as much as he'd thought. Nick knew how
hard this was for Abby. She had firsthand knowledge
of being on a shoestring budget, the only thing between
her and the wolves at the door.

Nick remembered a time he'd been in Abby's shoes,
professionally speaking. Tom Marchetti put his faith in
OJT, on-the-job-training. His dad believed that Nick's
advanced degree in business only proved that he was
capable of thinking. Each of his four sons had to learn
the business from the bottom up. Nick had gotten his
real education the summer his father had sent him to
Phoenix, to supervise the opening of the first restaurant
outside of California. His most lasting lesson had nothing to do with business, he recalled bitterly. His em-
pathy for an employee had led to his orientation in the
finer points of getting dumped, big-time, in a relationship. He would never forget it.

But that was his problem, not Abby's. The restaurant
where she was assistant manager was the first in the
Marchetti's chain, started twenty years before. Now the
area demographics were changing and impacting business in that location. He was only mildly surprised that
Abby had correctly guessed that was the reason he'd
been there today to evaluate. She was a sharp cookie,
with a very tender heart. She was just filling in, but
had gotten her baptism of fire by telling that young
father to go home early.

"So what are you going to do about the business?" he asked.

Startled, she met his gaze. "Me? I'm just the relief pitcher."

"Isn't it the reliever's job to save the game?"

She looked at him thoughtfully for several moments. "I guess paying employees for twiddling their thumbs is unacceptable?" she said, half-hopeful.

"It is. Short of giving money away, what can management do?"

She thought for a minute. "Figure out ways to bring in customers."

"That's right. You've been to a few management seminars. What did you learn?"

"Mission, vision, philosophy," she said without hesitation.

"Good, you can spout terminology. But what does it mean as far as Marchetti's Inc. is concerned?"

"Mission?" She thought for a moment. "'To provide high-quality, authentic Italian food at a reasonable cost, using customer-service skills to ensure clientele satisfaction,'" she recited.

At least someone read the company memos, he thought wryly.

"Okay, so you can memorize." He pointed at her. "What's the important part of what you just quoted?"

She frowned. "Which part?"

"Clientele. Do you know your customer base?"

"The area is older. First-time home buyers are moving in. That means primarily young couples, some with children, some without. Most on a budget."

"Right. How can you make them want to allocate some of their hard-earned, double-income dollars for a meal out?"

"Coupons, flyers, discounts. A special kids' night. Maybe an all-you-can-eat deal on traditionally slower nights."

"All good ideas," he said.

"But don't they deviate from the company vision—every restaurant is the same, right down to the menu?"

"That was my father's vision. Times have changed. We can, too. Especially if you factor in philosophy."

"Let the managers manage?"

He nodded. His three brothers were also involved in the family business. Joe was CEO in charge of personnel and hiring. "If my brother's done his job, every restaurant has a dynamite manager, in which case all we have to do is stand back and let him or her do what he or she does best."

"So if every location is made up of specific clientele, aspects of the operation could be altered accordingly?"

"Why not?" he asked. If every employee was like her, his job would be a snap. "Think about it, Abby."

"I will."

They grinned at each other for several moments. Nick hadn't felt this exhilarated in a long time and sensed that Abby felt it, too. Excitement flushed her cheeks and sparkled in her eyes. Her full lips turned up, revealing a rare, beautiful smile. He couldn't remember the last time talking business had been so much fun.

Then she blinked and her smile faltered. The serious, professional mask was replaced faster than you could say "fettuccine Alfredo."

She glanced at her watch. "Wow, look at the time. You're going to be late."

He suddenly had an idea. "Come to dinner with us."

Startled, she put a hand to her chest. "Me?"

He looked around. "I don't see anyone else here. Of course, you."

"I couldn't."

"Sure you could. Madison likes you. You admitted you like her. Give me one good reason why you can't join us."

"Okay. Car pool."

"Excuse me?"

"Sarah and her friends got a ride to the movies with April Petersen's mom and I have to pick them up."

He couldn't help wondering how many other things she'd missed because she'd become a mother at eighteen. He was helping her plan a milestone birthday for Sarah. Had anyone made hers special?

"What did you do when you turned twenty-one?"

She looked surprised, then shrugged. "I don't remember. I suppose the usual—school, took care of Sarah, and work."

"That's against the law."

"Huh?" she said.

"In my family there's a traditional rite of passage into adulthood that involves going somewhere your ID will be checked. An unforgettable experience."

"That's really nice, but I don't see—"

He grinned. "Obviously I owe you a twenty-first birthday."

Chapter Two

Abby blinked away her shock. He felt responsible for her twenty-first birthday? She wanted to ask where that had come from.

Instead she said, "Aside from the obvious, that it's now two years after the fact, why would you think you *owe* me that?"

"When you hired on, you became part of the Marchetti family. I don't know where my head was back then."

The dark look was back momentarily, as if he was remembering something unpleasant. He so rarely looked angry, she couldn't help noticing that it had happened twice in one day. What bad memory had brought that expression to his face? Whatever it was, she had the most absurd desire to make it better.

She pushed the thought away and said, "That's a no-brainer. Your head was where it always is." She gave him a wry look. "Buried in business."

"Maybe." One corner of his mouth lifted, replacing

his tension with teasing. "The fact is, you became an adult and the occasion was not properly acknowledged."

"It was a long time ago. I don't care—"

"I do," he said in his *I'm-the-boss* voice that suffered no pithy comeback.

"It's very nice of you to be concerned, Nick. But it's over. Even if I wanted you to, there's no way you can get that back for me."

Abby made a conscious effort to wear a blindfold when she looked back on her life. The past held mostly bad memories. But the future was full of possibilities, as soon as it was her turn.

He glanced at the watch on his wrist and stood up, grabbing his jacket as he did. "I don't have time to debate this right now. But you *will* have a birthday celebration."

"If it involves pointy hats and spin the bottle, count me out."

He laughed and opened the door. "Don't worry. I'll take care of everything."

Abby stood in the doorway, watching until his broad back was swallowed up by the darkness. She figured there wasn't too much danger of kissing games for her. Like all the other guys in her past who had tried to plan something with her, Nick would find out she had responsibilities that pushed her own dreams aside.

But the thought of something wild and unpredictable was exciting—for the second and a half she allowed herself to fantasize. Then she filed the daydream under "footloose and fancy-free," to be pulled out at a later, more convenient time.

Her turn would have to wait.

* * *

After dinner, Nick drove Madison home, then walked her to her front door. The building was in an exclusive area of town. This sophisticated high-security condo complex was exactly where a well-bred, up-and-coming female attorney should live.

Sometimes he forgot that Madison Wainright was in such a high-powered profession. She was petite, even smaller than Abby. The black knit dress she wore was a high-collared number that flared at mid-calf and hugged every curve in between. She chose clothes that she thought would make her look taller. From his vantage point she was woefully unsuccessful, since he was looking at the top of her red hair.

He preferred blue-eyed blondes. Although more important than the color of a woman's hair was her sense of humor. He recalled Abby's electronics-department comment about woofers and hooters. His mouth twitched again. She had said that on purpose. When she wasn't hiding behind her professional face, Abby was fun.

So was Madison. Usually. Although he had a feeling her sense of humor had taken the night off. It could be she was preoccupied with the case she was working on, but he suspected he'd done something besides pick her up late to put the wrinkle in her briefs.

At her front door, he stood one step below the porch while she put her key in the lock. The outside light spilled onto the step and sparkled in her green eyes as she glanced hopefully at him. "Would you like to come in for a nightcap?" she asked.

"I wish I could, but there's an early meeting tomorrow," he answered.

"Okay. Thanks for dinner." Her voice was brittle. She pushed the door open and started inside.

"What's wrong?"

"Nothing. Good night, Nick."

He moved beside her and put his hand on her arm. "Something's eating you. What is it?"

"We need to talk."

A shudder slithered through him. He had a feeling he wasn't the only man on earth who had that reaction to those words. But he figured he had a better reason than most. The last time a woman had said that to him, his life had turned upside down.

He took a deep breath and said, "Okay, shoot."

She hugged her black clutch purse to her chest. "You're going to dismiss everything I'm about to say, but it's time to say it. You don't have feelings for me, at least not the way I want you to. Although, when you picked me up tonight, I hoped things would be different."

"What are you talking about?"

"You were excited, practically humming with enthusiasm. I haven't seen you like that in weeks."

"I'm always upbeat, Madison. And of course I care about you."

"See? I knew you would dismiss me."

He stuck his hands in his pockets. "I'm not. I just don't understand where you're going with this."

"We hadn't finished our dinner salads before the other Nick was back, the one I can't reach because he's buried in business."

Funny, he thought. That's almost what Abby had said to him earlier. "You make me sound like a schizophrenic, Madison."

"You are. At least now you are. When we first met, you were attentive. You courted me. It's what made me fall—" She pulled herself up to her full five feet, one inch, a bit more with heels, and looked him in the eye. "Now you're like two people. The fun-loving Nick and the one who's only interested in profits over the last year. The latter is the guy I always see. I'm not sure I like him."

"Next you'll accuse me of having an evil twin."

"That's what it feels like."

"You're exaggerating—"

"Am I? Think about it, Nick."

He did, trying to remember, and came up empty. He put his hands on her waist and felt her stiffen. "I don't know what you're talking about."

She shook her head. "It's all right. This probably wasn't the right time to bring it up."

"I get the feeling you're holding something back."

She smiled a little sadly. "You're very perceptive when you want to be. I've been wondering lately if we shouldn't take a break from each other."

"Are you serious?"

"Yes. I saw the look in your eyes earlier when you explained that Abby Ridgeway was the reason you were late."

"That's right. Abby and I were talking business."

"That's not the way it looks to me. I suspect you have feelings for her that have nothing to do with business."

"Your imagination is working overtime," he said, a little hotly.

"Really?" Her chin lifted. "When's the last time you kissed me as if you really meant it?"

That stopped him cold. He thought back and came up empty. Then he tried to pull her into his arms. "We can remedy that," he suggested.

She stiffened again and refused to mold herself

against him. "If I have to remind you, it takes the magic out of the moment," she said.

"I've been preoccupied—"

She shook her head. "Like I said, this is the wrong time. I'm pretty beat. And I have to be in court early."

"All right." He hesitated. "How about a long weekend soon? To talk this through?"

"I don't think so."

Nick kissed her cheek. "I'll call you."

"You don't have to. Good night," she said. Moments later, she disappeared inside and he heard the dead bolt slide shut.

With his hands in his pockets, Nick slowly walked down the stairs to his car. The conversation with Madison had rattled his chain. Feelings for Abby? That was absurd. They were nothing more than friends.

He was perfectly content with Madison and things the way they were. She was an intelligent companion and did him proud when she accompanied him to business functions. But he *couldn't* remember the last time he'd *really* kissed her and to be honest, he hadn't missed it.

But Madison wanted more. She was a wonderful woman and deserved more. He'd come to a fork in the road. Or maybe it was more like facing the three doors on a game show.

Behind door number one was a question mark. Door number two was Madison. He liked and respected her. She was beautiful, brainy and would be an asset to any man. His parents admired her. More than once his mother had hinted that procrastination was dangerous. He grinned. *Hint* was the wrong word. Flo Marchetti had as much tact as a charging rhino. She'd come right out and asked him if he was waiting for divine instruction from the burning bush.

He'd given her some spin about not being ready to settle down. If he and Madison were right together, nothing would be changed by waiting. At the time, he'd believed that. But he sensed that he and Ms. Wainright had just experienced a fish-or-cut-bait situation. He'd bet his new red Corvette that she wanted a family vehicle. She wanted the M-word. Marriage.

The only M-word he could give her was maybe. After his sister married his best friend and his niece was born, he'd started thinking. What would it be like to come home to a special woman? Children? To have all the hours at work mean something in terms of having a family of his own. He'd thought about asking Madison to marry him. But the thought always made him want to run far and fast in the opposite direction.

Then there was door number three—life as he knew it. He had a dynamite career. Building the family business along with his brothers was about as good as it got. Family. An image of Abby jumped into his mind. They were friends. Madison was dead wrong about there being anything romantic between him and Abby. Hadn't he told her just a few hours before that she was practically a relative? As in a little sister.

He'd tried to be there for her over the years. At first he'd called regularly and dropped in on her and Sarah to make sure they were okay. Abby always put on a brave front. She only came to him in crisis situations. Or to connect cable and hook up her stereo, he thought with a grin. He'd stepped into the big-brother role, to watch over her. But work commitments and Abby herself prevented him from keeping tabs on her as he felt he should. Sarah wasn't shy about calling, but Abby was different. If not for the info her sister gave him, he wouldn't have a clue about how Abby spent her free time.

He teased her about not dating, but didn't really know what was holding her back. But that was a separate issue. Something else was bothering him now. He had told her tonight that she was practically a member of the family.

Some relative *he* was. Relatives didn't ignore a birthday as important as number twenty-one. He wondered if the world-famous greeting-card company had a sentiment for a situation like this.

He opened his car door and slipped behind the wheel. A greeting card wasn't good enough. A grand gesture was what he needed to wipe the slate clean. Then he would see about mending fences with Madison.

Abby heard the knock at her door. Annoyance trickled through her at the interruption. It was nine in the morning on her day off. She was up to her elbows in dust, wax and cleaning solutions. She had built up a head of steam and was prepared to scour the place from engine to caboose. But first she had to get rid of the door-to-door salesman.

She opened the door and said, "I'm not interested—"

Nick grinned down at her. "Hi. And how do you know you're not interested?"

"I thought you were selling something."

"Not exactly. Are you going to invite me in?"

"The place is a mess."

"Is it fatal?"

"Sarah and I have built up immunities." She returned his smile and opened the door wider. "Enter at your own risk."

"Thanks."

She rested her sweatpants-clad hip against the back of the love seat and folded her arms across her chest. "To what do I owe this visit? Is everything all right? Did the restaurant burn down? A fire in the kitchen? Mutiny in the ranks?"

His dark brows drew together. "Has anyone ever told you you're a glass-is-half-empty sort of person?"

"Yes. So before my imagination really gets revved up, you might want to tell me what you're doing here."

"I'd like to think it's a good thing." He looked down at her. "I'm here to invite you to dinner."

"Dinner?" Abby resisted her inclination to feel Nick's forehead for signs of fever and delirium.

What in the world was he thinking? Going out with the hired help? He was too young for a midlife crisis. Although she'd never seen that particular gleam in his eyes. And he wasn't wearing his customary suit. It was Saturday, but his reputation for working seven days a week was legendary. So she didn't often see him in casual clothes. And a good thing, too.

His jeans and the long-sleeved white shirt rolled to the elbows highlighted his masculinity. Casual clothes on Nick were dangerous to her unbreakable rule. Work attire was comfortable and safe. Besides reminding her that she needed to maintain a professional relationship, his suit jacket hid that great butt—

Whoa, Abby. Don't go there. This was shaky ground. He was her boss. She had no business critiquing his anatomy, even if it did kick up her heart rate. What was her world coming to?

No good. That's what. And not fair, since she was

dressed in gray sweats and no makeup, a scary proposition at best.

She pushed her hair out of her eyes. "I can't drop everything."

"You don't have to drop anything," he said. "In fact I recommend against dropping breakables."

"You know that's not what I meant. I have things to do."

He looked at his watch. "If I pick you up at seven-thirty, will that give you enough time?"

"There's never enough time," she said.

He shook his head sympathetically. "You need to have some fun, Ab."

"No, I don't." That came out so witchy. She sighed. "I don't mean to be rude, Nick, but just which part of *no* didn't you understand?"

"The *N* and the *O*." He folded his arms over his chest and grinned down at her.

"You know we could have had this conversation on the phone," she said.

"I had a feeling you would resist the idea. I thought it might take some convincing, and it's not as easy to get rid of me in person."

Abby let out a long breath. If she had known he *was* selling something, she would never have opened the door. And her day off had started out so well. She had formulated a plan. Life was so much easier that way. If she deviated from her daily goals, there would be more to do tomorrow. Her outline of the day hadn't included convincing Nick that she couldn't forget her responsibilities and go play with him.

"Let me explain this to you," she said. "*No* is a negative response to a proposition or situation. It means

I can't accompany you. But I appreciate the thought. It's very sweet—''

"Look at it this way, Ab. If you're going to do foot-loose and fancy-free someday, you need experience. You're the one who's facing the light at the end of the tunnel. Carefree abandon doesn't just happen. It needs single-minded training, determination, practice and sacrifice.''

"So going out to dinner is actually the first lesson in Footloose and Fancy-Free 101?''

"Yeah.'' He grinned. "The prerequisite is Spontaneity 100.''

She shook her head. "It's very nice of you, Nick. I'd rather do anything than search and destroy dust bunnies in this place,'' she said, grimly looking around her living room.

"But?'' he prompted.

"I have responsibilities. If I don't take care of them, my little boat will capsize. I have too much to do.''

"Name three things that will tank you if they're not done because you go out to dinner tonight,'' he said, confidence oozing from him.

It wasn't easy arguing with Mr. Perfect. If only his hair was sticking up in the back, or there was dirt on his handsome face or lettuce between his teeth. Anything that would put him on the level of someone like her. But that would never happen. He would always be at the head of the banquet table, and she would be in the corner trying to corral the dust bunnies.

"I'm waiting,'' he said. "Three reasons you can't throw caution to the wind and go with me.''

She had a sneaking suspicion he knew what she would say, and was prepared to bob and weave, and block her at every turn. "Okay. My classes.''

"It's Saturday. You don't have a class today."

"But I'm up to my ears in homework, and Sarah may have plans and need transportation."

"So do your homework this afternoon and I'll alert Ma to be on call with the Beamer for Sarah tonight. What's your third excuse?"

"The health department."

"What?"

"They're going to shut this place down if I don't clean it."

She squirmed uncomfortably when his black eyes narrowed on her. "You're reaching with that one. What are you afraid of, Abby? Me?"

"Of course not." That was only half-true. She *was* cautious of him, or rather spending time with him that wasn't work-related.

She understood work, and her place in the scheme of things. He was proposing a Cinderella scenario. Take her to dinner—translation, the ball. Let her have some fun and see how the other half lives. But at midnight the fairy tale would be over. He was right. She was afraid—to see the other side. Afraid of facing life after her matching horses and golden coach turned back into a pumpkin and dust bunnies.

Nick Marchetti was Prince Charming in a business suit. He was handsome, funny, and didn't have to worry about paying his electric bill if he used too much power during a heat wave. He was so far out of her league, it wasn't funny. When it was her turn at the plate, she wanted to swing away. She wanted to have fun. She wanted to date. She wanted enough time to nurture a budding relationship.

It wouldn't be easy to take the first step; so she would wait until her life simplified and she had the time to devote to a man. She had enough scars to convince her that unless she waited for her turn, the romance in her crystal ball was doomed to failure. When she had a clear field, she would give it a try. But what guy could compare favorably to Nick?

All of that wasn't the worst. What scared her most was that the delicate balance between work and friendship would be somehow altered. After her parents had died, she'd assumed adult responsibilities. She hadn't known how to handle the legal matters, let alone how or what to do with the house. Nick had stepped in and advised her. Besides her sister, their relationship was the brightest part of her life. Knowing he was there, whether she needed him or not, had gotten her through the rough times. She didn't want to jeopardize what they had.

"Look, pal, I'm only talking about a couple of hours. An evening. A belated twenty-first-birthday dinner. You would be doing me a favor."

"Oh, really." A grin broke through. She loved watching Maneuvering Marchetti in action. And what a stretch! Two and a half years after the fact, how was he going to turn her belated twenty-first birthday celebration to his advantage? "How?"

"Let me count the ways." He held his hand up and touched his index finger. "Number one—clear my conscience. Number two—make my star employee happy. A happy employee is a productive employee."

"So this is all about you?"

"Not entirely. You haven't heard number three yet."

"Okay. Lay it on me."

He held up three fingers and wiggled them. "If you don't lighten up and have a little fun, you're heading for a midlife crisis of astronomic proportions. As an honorary Marchetti," he said, pointing at her, "you're entitled to a free, all-expense-paid dinner where you will be instructed by yours truly in the finer art of celebrating a milestone birthday. While there, you will get a long-overdue lesson in having fun."

Temptation tugged at Abby and stirred something dormant in her soul. She longed to do something wild, something spontaneous and completely out of character. Her whole body vibrated with excitement. The prospect of plain Abby Ridgeway spending the evening with the fabulous Nick Marchetti was the stuff of fantasy.

Then her cautious, practical nature reared its ugly head and told her to turn him down.

"I don't know, Nick," she said, not quite able to listen and obey her sensible side.

"Then consider this—if you say no, I'm planning to throw you over my shoulder and carry you off. I thought you'd learned never to mess with a Marchetti determined to have his way." He sighed. "Somehow I suspected it would come down to brawn over rational thought."

Abby found she was leaning toward a yes, and it wasn't his phony threat of physical force. How could she turn him down? He seemed to want to do this and had taken steps to make it happen, including thinking of Sarah. A girl who said no would have to have her head examined.

"Then in an effort to preserve my dignity, the answer is—okay." Then she thought of something and said, "What should I wear?"

"A cocktail dress. This is an occasion for dressing up. I have a special place in mind."

She touched his arm, ignoring the tingle in her fingertips. "Thank you, Nick."

"No need to thank me. On top of the motivations I listed, there's one I left out. Ma says I've been working too hard and should have some fun. Maybe now she'll get off my back."

She met his gaze and gave him a stern look. "You're lucky to have her."

"That was a joke. Now I'll leave you to your responsibilities." He tapped her nose. "I'll pick you up at seven-thirty. Be here. Be ready. Be prepared. No excuses."

Chapter Three

"Oh, Nick—" Words failed Abby.

They had just been seated at a window table in an exclusive restaurant high above the San Fernando Valley, and she looked down at the lights.

"You like it?" he asked.

She smiled at him. "I'd sure hate to be responsible for the electric bill. But yes. It's wonderful." She gazed at the sight again. "It takes my breath away."

"Yeah," he said.

She darted a glance at him and realized he wasn't looking outside. He was staring at her. Her breath caught for the second time in thirty seconds, and it had nothing to do with the view and everything to do with the intensity in his gaze. He'd never looked at her like that before.

"Is something the matter?" she asked. "Lipstick on my teeth? Mascara under my eyes? Is the dress wrong?"

He shook his head. "You look just fine," he answered.

"Then why are you staring at me?"

"It's just—" He shrugged, a gesture that told her he didn't have the words. Maneuvering Marchetti always had the words, so this was a noteworthy occasion. Noteworthy good or bad, she wasn't sure.

"Just what?" she prompted. A personal compliment from her boss bent her rule. But heck, just for the evening she could relax. Couldn't she?

"You don't look like this at work," he finished lamely.

"Does that mean the outfit is okay?" It was the only decent dressy thing she owned. She'd worn the long-sleeved, short-skirted, black, lace-covered sheath to the company Christmas party the year before. Obviously he didn't remember. She ignored the prick of disappointment. It was better to overlook what you didn't understand, and couldn't do anything about even if you did.

Just then the waiter appeared. "Can I get you something from the bar?"

Nick ordered a Scotch. Abby asked for a glass of white wine.

The waiter cleared his throat, looking embarrassed. "Miss, may I see some identification, please?"

Stunned, Abby reached for her small clutch purse, grateful that she'd thought to bring her driver's license. She handed it over for his examination. Nodding he said, "I'll bring your drinks right away."

Abby glanced at Nick who had a cat-who-ate-the-canary expression on his face. "Okay," she said. "I get it. That's what you whispered to the maître d' when we walked in."

"I haven't a clue what you're talking about."

"Come clean, Nick. You put him up to asking me for ID."

"If this was really your twenty-first birthday, they would have done it on their own. You don't look much older than Sarah."

She wasn't sure she liked that. "Thanks, I think," she said ruefully. But his attention to the small detail warmed her heart.

The waiter returned and placed their drinks in front of them, then slipped away while they leisurely looked at the menu. Nick sipped his Scotch, then rested his forearms on the small circular table. "Why don't you date, Ab?"

Where had that question come from and did she really want to answer it? she wondered.

"How do you know I don't?" she asked evasively.

"Sarah gives me a regular update on the trials and tribulations of the Ridgeway sisters. She says you might as well be a nun."

"She's so boy-crazy." Abby laughed, shaking her head. "In her opinion, anything less than total preoccupation with the opposite sex means you must be convent bait. But I suppose I was the same way at her age."

"Sarah says you're making her wait to go out alone with a guy until she's sixteen," he said. "When did you start dating?"

"Sixteen. And then I couldn't go out alone. It had to be group activities." She toyed with the stem of her wineglass, turning it so that the pale liquid caught the candlelight. "At the time, I thought my parents were from the Dark Ages. Now I see their wisdom. But times have changed. Kids grow up much faster today. I worry so about Sarah, and I don't know if she'll listen to me. I wish my mom and dad were here.''

"Two parents and a united front are definitely the way to go, especially when you're raising a teenager.''

"Even when the two parents aren't exactly united,'' she said. If the accident hadn't taken their lives, her parents might have stayed together. If they'd gotten the chance, it was possible they could have worked out their problems. Now Abby would never know. Mostly she'd learned to deal with the guilt of her part in the accident. But every once in a while it snuck up on her.

"What does that mean?'' he asked, a puzzled frown creasing his forehead.

She shrugged. "Nothing. I love my sister. I want her to have all the advantages I didn't. I'll do my best to take care of her all by myself.''

"Like I said before—you've got me, pal. Dial M for Marchetti and I'm there.'' He grinned. "I'll help you keep Sarah in line. But you changed the subject. Why don't you date?''

"No time.'' She fiddled with the small cocktail napkin beneath her glass. "I had too much to do after Mom and Dad died.''

"You *never* went out?'' The shock on his face was almost comical. "But you were only eighteen.''

"I tried a couple of times. But it didn't work. Too complicated.'' She looked out the window, searching for a way to change the subject. "I'd like to discuss this plan I have for the restaurant—''

"Hold it.'' He held up one finger for silence. "Didn't I explain tonight's rules?'' When she shook her head, he continued. "Then let me do it now. We are friends out for the evening to have fun. There will be no discussion of work. Period.'' He sipped his drink. ''Now, tell me how dating was complicated.''

She thought back, dredging up the memories. The problem with dredging was that you brought up a lot of stuff better left stuck in the muck. Like the pain. But she knew there was no point in putting Nick off. When he wanted something, he was like a dog who wouldn't let go of his favorite bone.

She'd best get it over with. ''First of all, I needed a free period of time that coincided with my date's.''

''What else?''

''I had to find someone to watch Sarah and be able to afford to pay them.''

''Okay.'' There was no emotion in his voice, but he was frowning thoughtfully as if this was a newsflash to him. ''I have a feeling there's more.''

''I was working, going to school and taking care of my sister. She demanded a lot of time back then. It was pretty traumatic, losing both parents at once.''

''I can only imagine.'' He reached across the table and rested his hand over hers. Wrapping his strong fingers around her own, he brushed a delicate caress across her palm, then squeezed reassuringly.

She wanted to lose herself in the warmth of that tingle-evoking touch, but warned herself not to go there. He could tell himself from now till next Tuesday that they were buddies out on the town. But she couldn't—wouldn't—forget that he was head honcho of the corporation she worked for. And it wasn't her job she worried about. Nick wouldn't fire her unless she turned into a psycho-stalking embezzler, who couldn't assistant-manage her way out of a paper bag. She worried that their relationship would change. Until she could spare the time, there was no point in investing energy in anything that even remotely smacked of fascination, flirtation or infatuation.

In spite of her fears, she couldn't bring herself to move her hand away. This was one isolated night that teetered on the edge of magical. It was unlikely that she would ever do this again. What could it hurt to let him hold her hand?

"Sarah got hysterical if she lost sight of me," she continued, relaxing a bit. "There just never seemed a perfect time to go out. The few guys who had the courage to ask me eventually got tired of waiting for me to line my ducks up in a perfect row long enough for a fast-food dinner and a movie." She smiled brightly, hoping it camouflaged the pain. "Finally, they just gave up on me."

Time had passed, but apparently not enough. The memory still hurt. The shock of losing her parents. The loneliness when her friends stopped calling because she never had time for them. Working at the restaurant. Waiting tables for dating couples, young people in love. Knowing it couldn't happen for her.

Abby had made up her mind to put romance on a back burner until Sarah was in college. That hadn't happened yet.

Her tingles grew tingles when Nick gently squeezed her fingers again. "The best things in life are worth waiting for, Ab. Those guys were young and stupid."

Either his touch, or her few sips of wine had made her far too warm. She eased her fingers out of his hold and folded her hands, resting them on the table. "Were you ever young and stupid, Nick?"

His dark, unreadable expression clicked on. "Isn't everyone?" he asked.

Answering a question with a question always piqued

her curiosity. "I don't believe you ever made a mistake in your life."

"According to who?"

Again a question instead of an answer. "It's just an observation. You're so mature and responsible. You're the oldest of five. You take care of everyone. Instead of being born with a silver spoon in your mouth, I picture you with a tiny briefcase in your hand. Men like you aren't prone to impulsive, foolish decisions."

"Is that so?"

Bingo. Third time's the charm. This line of questioning was getting interesting. She rested her chin on her linked hands and stared at him as she embarked on a fishing expedition. "Your life is perfect. I can't believe you ever did anything stupid or foolish when you were young."

"I got married."

Nick couldn't believe he'd said that. But Abby's eyes grew wide, so he figured he must have.

"You're married?"

"Not anymore." He stared back at her for several moments, waiting for her to laugh, waiting for the pain, anger and humiliation to wash over him.

"Are you going to tell me about it, or just let it hang there?"

He wasn't sure why he'd blurted out his secret in the first place. Now that he had, he figured he owed her an explanation. "It was about five years ago, just before we met, when I was opening the restaurant in Phoenix. I hired a woman to hostess. She came highly recommended. For me it was love at first sight."

"What about her?"

"She was involved with someone. But he walked out on her when she discovered she was pregnant."

She frowned. "Jerk."

"Yeah. She confided in me, and I was crazy about her. I wanted to take care of her and the baby. I proposed and she accepted. We got married in Las Vegas."

"Then what happened?"

"Like the proverbial bad penny, the boyfriend turned up."

"A day late and a dollar short."

"Something like that. But she took him back." When Abby opened her mouth to protest, he held up his hand. "She felt it would be best to give him a chance, since he was the baby's father."

"So you divorced?"

He shook his head. He almost wished they had. "It's worse than that. She had the marriage annulled, as if it had never happened."

She stared at him for several moments, absorbing the information. "Good."

He stopped twirling his glass and met her gaze. "Good?"

"Absolutely. If she was too dumb to know what a great guy you are, a guy willing to love her and another man's baby, then I'm glad she cut you loose. She doesn't deserve you."

"I don't know about—"

"She did you a favor. And the annulment means you're free to marry again in the church."

He shook his head. "Not me. I'm a confirmed bachelor."

"So this is the reason you haven't proposed to Madison."

Wow, she sure didn't beat around the bush. But she'd nailed it. Madison was right that their relation-

ship had cooled because of a woman. But it wasn't
Abby.

"Do you blame me? The height of stupidity would
be to make the same mistake again," he said, the words
bitter on his tongue. Every time he thought about settling down, memories of that time gave him a sick
feeling in his gut. "Golden boy gets shafted. Then she
made it as if it never happened."

"I'm sorry you went through that, Nick." Abby put
her hand over his. "But here's something to think
about. You've seen the plaque on my wall—What
Doesn't Kill Me Will Make Me Stronger?"

He nodded, enjoying the feel of her small hand on
his. He wondered if this same gesture he'd made moments before had delivered even half the comfort that
she was sending his way now. "And your point is?"

"I'm saving a spot for the companion—When Life
Gives You Lemons, Make Lemonade. You're stronger
for having gone through what you did. A weaker man
would have curled up and turned his back on women.
But you didn't do that."

"No?" Then why did he feel so reluctant to com-
mit? It sure as hell reinforced his conviction to stay a
bachelor.

"No. The experience made you the man you are
today—sensitive, caring, loyal, supportive and strong."

"Strong like a bull," he said, raising his arm and
flexing his biceps.

She laughed. "That's my point. You never lose your
sense of humor. So you see, Nick, *she* might have been
young and stupid, but not you."

Nick blinked once, then grinned. Abby made him
feel ten feet tall. He wasn't sure why he'd told her this
deep, dark ancient history. Maybe because she'd been

through hell, and he knew she would understand. Maybe because he wanted to show her that she wasn't alone, that he'd been kicked in the butt, too. Despite what she thought, his life was far from perfect. Whatever the reason, when the words were out, he'd expected teasing and jokes. Instead, her solid, unwavering support made him feel better.

"Thanks for listening, Ab."

"You're welcome," she said, a soft smile teasing the corners of her full mouth.

He'd brought her to dinner, not expecting the evening to be anything out of the ordinary. Boy was he wrong. The problem was, now he was having trouble taking his eyes from her lips, and thinking about how soft they looked.

But this night was not supposed to be about him. It was her celebration. "Enough about serious stuff. I promised to teach you how to relax and have fun."

His sudden grin, so attractive and sexy as sin, made Abby thank the gods that she was sitting down. It disarmed her so instantly and thoroughly that she realized she was way out of her league.

He continued to smile at her, and the wattage in his expression energized the butterflies in her stomach. It was impossible to think straight or function efficiently when he looked at her like that. Thank goodness he didn't do it much, and she didn't see him often at work. She would have been canned a long time ago. Which was as fine a reason as any to keep their relationship status quo.

She laughed and hoped he didn't notice it was just this side of shaky. "Yes, you did promise to teach me about fun. And you're a wonderful instructor. I've had such a good time tonight. I can't remember when I've

been so relaxed." She was babbling, and couldn't seem
to stop. "What more could there possibly be to learn?"

He stood up. "May I have this dance?"

"Dance?" That shocked her into semi-muteness.
Doggone him. Every time she barely got her boat on a
straight and narrow course, he rocked it.

"Yes, dance. Is there a problem?"

She shook her head. "It's just that this is a sort of
retrospective celebration. I thought you were talking
about a less mature and sophisticated kind of fun."

"Like what?"

"I don't know. Water balloons from the balcony.
Shaving cream on the windows. Toilet paper the park-
ing attendant. That kind of fun."

"I take it you never did that stuff."

"No. Did you?"

"I refuse to answer on the grounds that I'm the
boss."

"I'll take that as a yes."

The band started a ballad. "C'mon, pal. Let's
boogie. Unless you're afraid to have too much fun."

He held out his hand, and Abby knew she couldn't
refuse without an explanation. The only one she had,
she wasn't about to share with him. She put her fingers
in his palm. "If you step on my toes, class is dis-
missed," she mumbled.

"Don't fret, Ab. I promise you'll enjoy this lesson."
His voice, as deep and smooth and seductive as expensive brandy, made her skin warm from head to toe.

Dancing with Nick was a bad idea.

He led her onto the floor where several other couples
were gliding in time to the music. Facing her, Nick put
his hand on her waist, pulling her close to his muscular
length. The fragrance of his aftershave was wonderful,

masculine and just plain *wow*. The next thing she
knew, she had a weird nervous sort of feeling in her
stomach.

Then he gripped her hand and started to move in the
steps of a waltz. Abby put her hand on his shoulder. It
was either that, or let her arm dangle at her side, which
would surely earn her some curious stares. Nick held
her loosely, but as they circled the floor, their bodies
bumped and brushed, sending sparks through her. As
more couples joined them, and the area grew crowded,
Nick tightened his hold on her, keeping her next to his
solid strength. He sort of hunched forward, as if he was
surrounding her, protecting her. They were pressed
close from chest to knee and Abby could hardly
breathe.

She wished she could stay like this forever.

She was lulled by the music, the atmosphere. Se-
duced by wine and song. Not to mention the man every
other woman in the room kept staring at. And he was
Abby's.

No.

Not hers. Just her escort. Her friend. Her boss. She
sighed. This was too complicated. She longed for the
serenity of work. She wouldn't venture out of her comfort zone again.

Then she remembered Sarah's party. She would have
to venture out for that. Or rather let Nick in. Just once
more. Then back to her ironclad rule.

A few weeks from now, her commitments involving
Nick Marchetti would be over and done with. End of
fairy tale. Cinderella could go back to her corner without her happy ending. Life could get back to normal.
Just the way she liked it.

So why did the thought of that make her so sad?

* * *

"How do you think it's going?" Abby asked.

Nick looked down at her, nervously twisting her fingers together as she watched the teenage party in her apartment. He stood beside her on the patio, monitoring the group through the sliding glass door. In her blue jeans and white sweater, she hardly looked older than the kids.

A vision flashed through his mind, of her in that sexy black dress when he'd wined and dined her. He hadn't planned to blurt out his secret, and ever since had analyzed why he'd done it. Maybe he'd just needed to finally unburden himself, and she'd been handy. Or more likely it was the fact that she'd been knocked around by life and his gut told him she would understand. Whatever. He hadn't expected the night to be anything special, but he'd told her something no one in his family knew. Her bracing words had meant a lot to him.

And as if that weren't enough, he'd seen her in a way he never had before. More than once since then, the seductive image of her in that dynamite dress had skewed his train of thought. Usually at the most inconvenient time. Or he'd get a whiff of perfume that would instantly produce a mental picture of Abby—from her sweet smile that reminded him of her innocence and made him want to protect her, to her wicked grin that made him just want her.

That night, Abby had opened up to him, too. She'd reminded him how gutsy she was, telling him a little more about her past. Like the difficulties of being a single parent to Sarah. What it had cost her to do the right thing. He found he was glad to have Abby in his life. He'd never thought about it before, but she'd come into his life right after his fiasco in Phoenix, when he'd sworn off women. Something about her had gotten to him. But he'd seen her as hardly more than a child who needed help. Now she was a woman. Was she ever!

He stifled that thought. He valued her friendship. He admired her courage, as well as her determination to give her sister the carefree life she'd lost when her parents had died.

As his thoughts turned to Sarah, he looked for her inside. A blond, blue-eyed younger version of Abby, she was huddled in the kitchen, whispering with three girls. Several guys sprawled on the couches in the apartment's tiny living room. In all, he'd counted ten teenagers, six boys and four girls. Abby had asked him how he thought the party was going. He felt *party* was too strong a word for the activity he saw.

But he said confidently, "I think it's going fine."

Abby met his gaze and her forehead wrinkled with worry. "You're right," she wailed. "It's a disaster. Girls in the kitchen, guys in the living room. A sweet-sixteen extravaganza she'll never forget," she said.

"It's not that bad. At least we can see them all." He quickly counted heads. "Except the pushy little twerp who's on the phone in your bedroom."

"Yeah. James. If he's on the phone to Japan, his mother and I are going to have a dialogue."

"He's not the one Sarah has a crush on, I hope?"

She shook her head. "See the cute guy on the end of the couch closest to the TV? The one with the adorable dimple in his chin?"

"I have no frame of reference for 'cute' and 'adorable,' but I believe I know who you mean."

"That's Austin Reese. He's the one she'd like to be

her main squeeze, or whatever terminology they're using now for a significant other.''

"I believe the term is 'going out.' What do you know about him?''

"He's an honors student and captain of the football team.''

"Is that all? Maybe I should have Steve run a background check.'' Steve Schafer was his best friend and his younger sister's husband. Nick knew he would be happy to help. It was his business, and he made a good living doing executive background checks for major corporations. A teenage honors student should be a piece of cake.

"I don't think that will be necessary.'' She frowned. "I'm more concerned about getting through tonight without breaking her heart. She's been looking forward to this party for so long. She'll be devastated if it's a flop.''

Abby put her hand on his arm, an uncharacteristically familiar gesture. Probably a testament to how anxious she was. Abby never forgot herself. Even when she'd been in his arms dancing, he'd felt her struggle to maintain distance. Something between them simmered below the surface and she kept throwing ice cubes on it. Although his head warned him away, her reluctance tweaked his desire to explore the feeling. But not now. This was Sarah's night, and it was dying a slow death.

"It's time to bring out the big guns, Ab.''

"No kissing, Nick.''

"Who said anything about spin the bottle?'' He opened the screen door and stepped into the living room. The teenagers hardly noticed. Godawful music blared from Sarah's new CD player.

Nick crossed the space to the corner of the dining room where he'd left his ultimate weapon. He pulled the cardboard-boxed game from the bag.

"What's that?" Sarah asked.

"Twister," he answered. He walked over to the couch and tapped Austin on the shoulder. "Help me move this sofa out of the way." He pointed to the two teenage boys on the other couch. "You guys push that back, and the rest of you shove the coffee table in the corner."

A low-pitched grumbling started, but the kids followed his directions until the center of the room was empty. The game was nothing more than a plastic sheet containing four rows of different-colored circles and a spinner with corresponding colors that directed the participants where to put their hands and feet. The object of the game was to see how far and in what positions the players could contort their bodies before collapsing. Last one standing was the winner.

"Who's first?" Nick looked around the room and noted a general reluctance. This was unacceptable. He hadn't sat through hours of motivational business seminars for nothing, he thought grimly.

"If I don't get volunteers, I'll appoint someone." Still no takers. "Okay. Sarah. Austin. You're up."

Sarah's eyes widened. "Nick, I—"

"Let's go for it," the cute, adorably dimpled object of her affection said.

Austin Reese might just pass one of Steve's background checks after all, Nick thought approvingly. The two teenagers took off their shoes and stood on opposite sides of the mat while the rest of the group encircled them.

Nick hollered down the hallway. "James? Get in here! This is a party."

When the sandy-haired teen sheepishly materialized, Nick handed him the spinner. "Twirl the arrow. Wherever it stops, read the color and words. Think you can handle that?"

"No problem," the boy said.

"Good." He looked around. "Go," he said.

James did as he was told, then called out, "Right hand green."

Sarah and Austin bent to follow the directive. The next move was left foot red. They struggled to position themselves and started laughing. The other kids closed in around them and started calling out strategy.

Nick moved back to Abby, who was standing just inside the sliding glass door. The teenagers quickly got into the spirit of the game. When Austin fell, Sarah was the winner and another boy and girl clamored to play.

For the second time that night Abby put her hand on his arm. Instead of being anxious this time, she was grateful. "You're a genius, Nick. What a wonderful icebreaker. And no kissing."

"Like I said, dial M for Marchetti. Problems resolved. Crises averted. Flops fixed." He grinned down at her, but she was intently watching the game.

Fascinated, she moved forward and worked her way between James and another boy so that she could see what was going on. Nick followed her.

"Haven't you seen this before?" he asked.

She shook her head. "No. It looks like a lot of fun."

"It is," he answered.

Just then the two players fell, laughing. James looked at her and said, "Abby, it's your turn."

"No. This is for you guys."

"Go ahead, Abby." Sarah clapped her hands. "You and Nick try it."

Abby shook her head. "We're just here to watch."

Nick thought it might be fun. "C'mon, pal. Spontaneity 100, the refresher course. Let's show these young whippersnappers how limber us gummers are."

"Okay. You're on." She took off her sneakers and stood on the mat, staring at him expectantly.

Excitement sparkled in her eyes and flushed her cheeks a becoming pink. The fragrance of her perfume surrounded him making his pulse skip. Before he had time to explore any more of the effects she had on his senses, James spun the needle.

"Right foot green," he said.

They moved to obey and Abby grinned wickedly. "This is where sitting behind a desk all day is going to hurt you, Nick."

"Cheap talk, pal."

"Right hand blue," James said.

They squatted to comply, and he watched her blue eyes darken with determination. The teenager called out commands, and they followed his directions.

"Hey, are you guys going out?" James asked as he spun the needle.

"No," Abby snapped, a little out of breath from the exertion of the game. "He's my boss."

"Left foot yellow." James watched them move, studying the intimate position of their bodies after that last command. "You look like you're going out."

"Well we're not," Abby said breathlessly.

"Oh. Okay." He moved the spinner and called out, "Right hand red."

Abby groaned. The only way she could go without

winding up a human pretzel was on her back. Slowly, she maneuvered her body, then waited for him. Nick assessed his best move, then hesitated. If he took it, he would be on top of Abby in a very intimate position. A sense of challenge to undermine the distance she put between them dared him. He'd never been able to resist a dare.

He twisted his body over hers and put his hand on the dot. "There."

"James, spin the needle," she ordered. "Quick."

To the kids, her desperate tone could be a reaction to her precarious position in relation to the game. Nick wondered if it was more about her closeness to him.

He felt her breath on his cheek. Their mouths were half an inch apart.

"Hey, Nick," James said. "Why don't you kiss her?"

Abby looked at his mouth and her eyes widened slightly.

Nick had thought a lot about her full lips ever since that night at dinner.

"Yeah, kiss her." It was a girl's voice, but he couldn't see which one.

Suddenly, all the teenagers began to chant, "Kiss her. Kiss her."

He teetered between his need to protect Abby, his responsibility as a chaperone and role model and his macho standing with the guys.

Abby stared into his eyes and shook her head slightly, but he could see the pulse point throbbing in her neck. Nick found he wanted very much to know the texture, touch, and taste of her lips. What harm could a chaste little kiss do?

A lot, he decided reluctantly. "Sorry, guys. It's against the rules."

Chapter Four

"The rules?" Abby said, dazed and annoyed. Which was only slightly better than dazed and confused.

"Yeah," Nick answered. "Remember when you told me we have to put gay abandon on hold? A teenage party calls for a stick-in-the-mud mentality."

Abby knew there had to be a reasonable balance between stick-in-the-mud and gay abandon. Her heart hammered painfully. And if she could only catch her breath, she would figure out how to find that balance. Nick was right. She had laid down the "no kissing" rules. She had no right to be angry because he'd listened to her. But how was she to know that they would wind up in an intimate position and she would *want* him to kiss her?

"Hey. You guys are hogging the game." James looked at her.

"I guess he told us." She met Nick's amused gaze. "From one game-hog to another, do you think we should give someone else a turn?"

With one smooth, athletic motion he levered himself off her, got to his feet and reached a hand down. Automatically Abby grabbed it, then wished she hadn't as the warmth and strength of his touch sent more tingles of awareness through her. She let him help her up and quickly pulled her fingers away.

As soon as they moved, two of the teenagers took their place on the Twister mat. Turning her back on Nick, Abby walked to the slider, opened it, went out onto the patio, then firmly closed the door behind her. At first, the chilly November air cooled her hot cheeks. Then she started to shiver.

Was it just the cold night? Or, more disturbing, the absence of Nick's warmth, the loss of his masculine form pressed to her, the feeling of loneliness that crept in without his closeness? She stared at the lighted walkway that meandered past her apartment and through the entire complex. Things were beginning to spiral out of her control. When had that happened? How? *Why?*

Behind her, she heard the door slide open, then closed. Without turning she knew who had joined her.

"Something wrong, Ab?" Nick asked, his deep voice raising goose bumps from head to toe on her body.

"No."

At least nothing that a double dip in a frigid stream wouldn't cure. With a shock, she realized something quite astonishing.

Nick was the first man she had ever almost kissed.

Technically it wasn't her first time, but the kisser had been a boy. Nick was a man. Somehow she knew he would have done the deed with confidence, finesse and thoroughness. He'd made her pulse pound, her heart race and stolen the breath from her lungs without even touching his mouth to hers. Oh, how she wished he had!

If she wasn't careful, he would see that. What if he took her up on the invitation? She would be out of the frying pan into the fire.

How could she keep him from seeing how very much she wanted to feel his lips pressed to hers? *You're being stupid,* her inner voice scolded. Why would he kiss her when he had Madison Wainright? She shivered and rubbed her arms.

"You cold?" he asked.

"A little. I think I'll go back inside," she said, turning.

He pulled off his plaid flannel shirt. Underneath, he wore a black T-shirt that molded to the masculine contours of his chest and flat belly even as it pulled tight around the muscles of his upper arms. Casual clothes merely enhanced his considerable manly charms. And why did that T-shirt have to be black? It gave him just a hint of irresistible bad-boy appeal that made her knees weak. New rule—and it was now number one— never see him outside of work where it was okay to dress casual. And at work... All she could do was hope and pray that she didn't see him much. And when she did, with luck, this puzzling attraction would be gone.

He slipped his body-warmed shirt around her shoulders. "Let's talk a minute."

"About?" she asked, permitting herself just a second or two to savor the wonderful scent of the aftershave that would forever remind her of Nick.

"What just happened."

Did he mean the near-miss kiss? She hoped not. If he insisted on a discussion, she couldn't possibly keep him from knowing she wanted him to do it. If only she was as good at maneuvering as he was. She needed a diversion, a smoke screen of monumental proportions.

"There's nothing to talk about," she hedged. *Wow. Way to go, Ridgeway.* That was some impressive evasive action. The United States special forces could use you on covert missions.

"I'd believe that if I didn't think you were afraid of something. What is it, Ab?" His voice was gentle and kind.

"I'm not afraid of anything," she answered. This was no time for him to be nice to her. And vice versa, she thought. "I was just wondering what Madison would think about this whole thing."

"What whole thing?" he asked. She could almost hear the click of the On switch as his dark eyes ignited with interest.

She thought for a moment. "To anyone looking on, it might appear that there was something of a personal nature between us."

"Is there?" he asked, his mouth quirking up.

She decided to ignore the question. "Someone who didn't know us might think we shared something besides a work relationship. We both know that's absurd. But if Madison had been here, what would she have thought?"

A wary look narrowed his eyes. "That we're incredibly limber for two old people."

"Be serious, Nick." It scared her that he didn't look as if he was joking. That made her determined to put a lighter spin on this discussion, at least until she could get herself out of it without looking like a fool. "You don't think that she might think that she might not be the right woman for you if you could almost kiss another woman?"

One corner of his mouth lifted. "It's scary that I understand what you just said. I kiss my mother and sister and she doesn't think anything of it."

Abby breathed a sigh that was two parts relief and one part regret. Nick put her in the same category as the women in his family. She desperately wanted to believe that.

"Now that I think about it," she said, "why didn't Madison come to the party? You did ask her?"

He hesitated a moment. "Yes."

"And?"

"She couldn't make it," he said.

Abby tilted her head as she looked at him. "Why?"

"I don't know," he answered. "She didn't return my calls."

Her face took on a sober expression. "Oh, Nick. What happened? Did you have a fight?"

"Not exactly. We had a talk, and since then she's been avoiding me."

"It sounds like she's trying to let you down easy," Abby said.

"Could be."

"But why? Madison Wainright is smart. She knows a good thing when she sees it."

He crossed his arms over his chest, tucked his fingertips under his arms and studied her. She met his gaze almost defiantly.

"There may be a reason Madison is trying to let me down easy."

"What could that be?"

"You."

"Don't be ridiculous!"

"Some women think I'm passably good-looking and

reasonably intelligent, with an above-average sense of humor. What do you find so ludicrous?''

"It's not you. I'm the one who wouldn't pass muster."

"Says who?"

Before she could answer the question, Sarah opened the slider and poked her head out. "Help, Nick," she called in a loud whisper. "The party's dying. Did you bring any more games?"

He looked at Abby. "We'll discuss this later, at a mutually convenient time. Right now I have teenagers to entertain, a party to save."

"Superman's got nothing on you," she said dryly. "There's no phone booth handy. Feel free to use my bedroom to change into your superhero ensemble. A cape and tights." She sighed and laid a hand on her chest. "Be still my heart."

"You really have to get out more, Ab. The phone booth is ancient history. Now I use the old spin and switch." He flashed her a grin before going inside to rescue the party.

A week later, Nick passed through the dining room in Abby's restaurant. He glanced at his watch and noted that it was 10:30 a.m. Not long before the lunch crunch. He'd seen her in action during the busy time. Perpetual motion. She did everything from seating customers to clearing off tables. No job too big or too small. He wondered if he'd subconsciously timed this business visit so that he'd have a chance to talk to her when she wasn't overwhelmed with customers. There hadn't been a mutually convenient time to continue the discussion begun the night of the party.

In fact, he hadn't seen her since that night. He won-

dered if she'd given him a passing thought. He hadn't
forgotten a single detail of that evening, especially
wanting to kiss her. When he'd seen Abby under the
stars, with the moonlight turning her hair to silver, he
was reminded of what Madison had said. That he had
decidedly unbusinesslike feelings for her. Is that why
he'd confided something to her he hadn't shared with
anyone else? He grinned, remembering the time he'd
told her that guys always wanted what they couldn't
have. He was living proof of that theory. Which was
why he wanted to initiate a dialogue with the enigmatic
Miss Ridgeway and not be interrupted by her dedicated
work ethic and the lunch bunch. He planned to do his
best to make this a mutually convenient time for both
of them.

He figured he'd find her doing paperwork in the office and headed past the kitchen, with its delicious gar-
lic and marinara-sauce smells, to the rear of the building. Even before he reached the doorway, he heard
angry voices. Correction: one angry voice. Sarah was
there and if the decibel level of her words was any
indication, she wasn't a happy camper.

"You always say no without even thinking about
it," she wailed. "You want me to be like you—no
friends, no fun, no life. A withered-up old maid."

Nick was about to enter the room when the teenage
girl hurried out, then turned into the hall and collided
with him. He steadied her and she looked up at him,
the sheen of tears in her eyes.

"What's wrong, kiddo?"

"Ask *her*," she said angrily, glancing over her
shoulder. "I want to go on a snow trip to the mountains
on Thanksgiving weekend, and she said no without
even thinking about it. She always says no. She never

lets me do anything. Help me, Nick." Her tone was loud enough to carry into Abby's office.

"How did you get here? Aren't you supposed to be in school?" he asked, stalling. Abby might have very good reasons for saying no. If so, he didn't want to interfere.

"It's a holiday. They let us have them every once in a while. And as for how I got here—" She broke off and glanced over her shoulder again. When she spoke, her voice was lower, so that only he could hear. "Don't tell her or she'll freak. She thinks I came on the bus. But my friend Stacy drove me. She got her driver's license last week." Anger suffused her blue eyes again. "I don't have a prayer of learning to drive a car."

"Don't borrow trouble, kiddo." He encircled her shoulders with his arm and gave her a quick hug. "I'll talk to Abby."

"Convince her to say yes," she said.

"No promises. I'm only going to talk to her."

Sarah nodded. "Thanks, Nick. You're a lifesaver. You're the best."

Before he could tell her not to count her chickens too soon, she was gone. He took a deep breath and walked into Abby's office.

"Hi, pal."

Abby sat behind the desk, her blue eyes flashing with anger. She tapped a pencil so fast and hard, any second he expected it to snap. "Don't call me 'pal.' A pal wouldn't have gone over to the other side. You're a traitor."

Abby must be really upset to forget that it was politically incorrect to call your boss names. "You heard?"

"There's no way you're changing my mind," she said by way of an answer.

"I said I'd talk to you. Did it ever occur to you that I might agree with your decision? Jumping to conclusions has reached epidemic proportions today. Or is it just the Ridgeway sisters?"

"She wants to go away for three days."

"The impertinence! Off with her head."

"It's not funny, Nick."

"Okay. Is she going with a guy?"

Apprehension chased the anger from her eyes. "Oh, Lord, I never thought of that. She said it's a church group activity."

"Then I'm sure it is. I didn't mean to supply you with grist for the worry mill."

"She said there will be adult chaperones."

"That explains it."

"What?" she asked suspiciously.

"Why you told her no."

"I should have known you'd take her side. It's up in the mountains, Nick. What if it's awful and she wants to come home? There could be snow on the roads. She could do herself bodily harm on the ski slopes. She's never skied before. What if—"

"Friends and snow and skis, oh my."

"You're impossible." She glared at him. "In spite of what she thinks, I don't always say no without giving the matter some thought." She fiddled with the pencil in her hands. "I know she didn't mention that I suggested to her that I go along as one of the chaperones?"

"No."

"See. You take her side without even hearing what I have to say."

"Okay. I'll admit she momentarily got the sympathy vote. What did she say to your compromise?" He had a pretty good idea, but for the sake of diplomacy, he wanted to hear it from Abby.

"I love my sister, and I don't want her to get hurt."

He folded his arms over his chest as he lounged in the doorway. If she kept skirting his questions, they could be here for a while. "I understand. But that's not what I asked."

Abby sighed, a big dejected sound. "She said she would rather sprout a zit the size of Texas on her nose than have me along as one of the chaperones."

"It's a shame that girl hasn't learned to speak her mind," he said shaking his head sympathetically.

"This is nothing to joke about, Nick."

"At the risk of upsetting you, I think it is. You need to lighten up, Ab. Sooner or later you have to let her try out her wings. What better way than with adult supervision? I don't understand what's bothering you."

She set her elbows on her paper-strewn desk and rested her chin in her palms. The gloomy pose was very childlike in spite of all her adult responsibilities.

"Then I'll explain to you what's bothering me," she said. "The mountains are several hours away by car. I don't like being so far away from Sarah in case she needs me."

Nick decided not to point out that Abby was counting the days until Sarah went away to college. There was a better-than-even chance that big sister wouldn't be allowed to tag along. Then she would be forced to let go. He was concerned that if Abby didn't cut Sarah some slack, there would be rebellion more serious than hiding the fact that she was riding around with a recently licensed driver. Nick understood Abby's fear.

She'd lost both parents when they had left on a pleasure trip. But life went on. Under the circumstances, he had to agree with Sarah. His problem was finding a diplomatic way to tell Abby.

"Why don't you contact the trip coordinator to confirm Sarah's information?"

"I plan to," she said. "But that won't completely ease my mind."

"Where are they going?" he asked.

"San Bernardino mountains. Big Bear."

"That's where the family cabin is." He might just have the beginnings of a solution. "Why don't you use it that weekend?"

She looked startled. "I couldn't."

Was Sarah right? Did Abby always say no without giving thought to the situation?

"Why not?"

"What about work?" she asked.

He looked down at the papers on her desk. "Isn't that the schedule you're working on?" When she nodded he said, "Mark yourself off."

"I'm not sure that's fair. I—"

"If Sarah had agreed to your chaperone solution, you'd have had to. Why not throw caution to the wind and do it? You can quietly let the trip supervisors know where to reach you. It will give you some peace of mind and Sarah some independence. It's a win-win situation for everyone. Especially me. I get to be the guy who made two women happy."

"Not so fast. I can't pay you for it. My budget is limited—"

"Who said anything about money?" A spark of anger sizzled inside him. "I offered it to you as a favor."

"But that wouldn't be professional. You're my boss. People would talk."

"Not even the world's largest roll of duct tape would stop that," he said, peeved at her. She was throwing up hurdles where there didn't need to be any. "It doesn't matter what people say. There's nothing going on between us." *Liar,* a voice in his head piped up. But he didn't want to go there. "I'm your friend."

"I hope so," Abby said.

Did she? He couldn't shake the feeling that she was trying to keep him from getting close. He continued to stare at her and noticed that her chin lifted a little, as if she were fighting some inner struggle.

She looked down at the pencil in her hands. "Sarah and I value your friendship, and it wouldn't be right to take advantage of that."

"It's not taking advantage if I offer."

"Then why does it feel that way?" she asked.

When did it get to be a major pain in the butt to do something nice for a friend? "Would it make you feel better if I have Luke dock your paycheck by five dollars a week for the next two years?"

"If I could spare that five dollars, it would make me feel a lot better. But I can't, Nick."

"Then consider it a bonus for my most valued employee."

"I don't take charity."

He shook his head as if trying to clear it. "Excuse me? When did you stop working?"

"I haven't. But what does that have to do with anything?"

"Employee bonuses are a common business practice. Happy workers are productive workers. Charity is a handout."

"You're making that up, or at the very least stretching the facts."

"I'm not. Scout's honor," he said, holding his hand up, palm out. "In fact, you would be doing us a favor. The place doesn't get used much anymore." He was making *that* up. "Someone needs to go up and check that the roof hasn't fallen in and the plumbing still plumbs."

"Really?" She didn't look completely convinced, but she was weakening.

"Yeah," he said confidently.

"If you're sure, it would be a lifesaver. Sarah really wants to go on the trip. And I'd feel a lot better if I was close by."

"Consider it done."

"Thanks, Nick. I really appreciate it. I'll call Sarah in a few minutes. She'll be so excited. The bus should have let her off at home by then."

He wondered if he should tell her about Sarah's actual transportation indiscretion. He decided against it, but made a mental note that during his next conversation with the teenager in question, he would make her promise to fess up. Since he had a feeling the schedule of a teenage driver might allow for more side trips than public transportation, he didn't want Abby to find that Sarah wasn't home yet. Big sister would worry.

He thought of the perfect way to distract her. The beauty was that it was reason number two for his visit.

"So, now can we talk about what almost happened at the party?"

Chapter Five

"What would that be?" Abby asked.

"Very funny, pal. I think you know very well what that would be," he said.

Her heartbeat went from normal to off the scale in a split second. She *did* know all too well what he meant. The exact moment when he almost kissed her. Since intimate encounters for her were nonexistent, creating a long lonely dry spell, near-kisses tended to stand out. Which, she rationalized, was exactly the reason she'd thought of little else since that night.

But she would rather have walked barefoot on hot coals than tell him as much. He'd been good to her and Sarah. Case in point: his offer of the family cabin so she could keep a watchful yet distant eye on her sister. That was above and beyond the call of duty for a boss.

What he wanted to talk about was the kiss that never was. More important—it never could be. Things might be different if she had the time, but she didn't. Not right now. And, if there was a God, eagle-eye Marchetti would not notice the blush that had crept into her cheeks when he'd mentioned the party. No way did she want to talk about that night. It would be too easy for the information to slip out that she had wanted him to kiss her.

So badly it had taken a very long time for the ache to go away.

When she continued to make herself stare at him blankly, he stopped leaning casually in the doorway and moved toward her like a determined predator stalking his prey. He passed through the invisible wall of her comfort zone, then had the nerve to sit on the corner of her desk. It was a blatantly masculine pose that tweaked every feminine response within her. She reminded herself again that his charm didn't affect her. Never had; never would.

One of his dark eyebrows lifted. "You're putting me on. You don't know what almost happened?"

"You mean at Sarah's party?"

"Of course I mean at Sarah's party. You. Me. A Twister mat." He snapped his fingers. "Anything coming to you yet?"

Did it bother him that she might have forgotten? Or worse—that she hadn't noticed? What would he think if he knew her mind drifted back to that moment countless times a day? No way would he drop the subject. *That's* what he would think!

"Of course," she said, as if she'd just remembered. Keep it light, she told herself. "Lesson number two of Footloose and Fancy Free 101. I forgot to thank you. My apologies, professor."

"You don't seriously think that's what this is about?" he asked frowning.

She nodded enthusiastically. "And I want you to know how much I appreciate it. A girl like me can't have too much preparation for the constantly changing dating scene. I still have a while yet before becoming an active participant. But when I need a crash refresher course, I'll be sure and let you know."

"Good," he said, a slight edge to his voice.

"Actually I'm glad you're here. I've worked up those ideas we talked about—"

Just then the beeper on his belt started a piercing wail. He pressed a button and checked the number.

"A crisis?" she asked. "Someone need rescuing, Superman?"

He frowned. "It's my mother. Can I use your phone?"

"Sure."

He came around the desk, stood beside her and placed his call. Abby moved her chair back, something she hoped looked like a polite attempt to give him space. In reality, it was the closest she could get to a full retreat. Running far and fast to a place where his warmth and masculine scent wouldn't start a fluttering in her stomach like a battalion of hummingbirds. What a pitiful attempt. She would need at least a county between them to do that.

"Hey, beautiful. What's going on?" he asked.

Abby watched his face. His tone was teasing and flirtatious. But his features softened with warmth and fondness that she somehow knew was reserved for his mother. Their conversation was short, then he said his goodbyes and hung up the phone.

Nick looked at her. "I have to go. I'm taking my mother to lunch. That was my reminder."

"You'd forget a lunch date with your mother?"

"No. But she says when you've raised someone from birth, it's hard to forget the times they screwed up."

"You're lucky," she said wistfully.

He wrinkled his brow. "That I messed up?"

"That you have the opportunity to spend time with your mom."

His face softened with sympathy. "I sometimes forget that the two most important people in your life were suddenly taken away. You still miss your parents." It wasn't a question.

"Yes."

"You can borrow mine," he offered. "Take the heat off the Marchetti brothers. We'd thank you for it."

"Thanks. I'll keep that in mind."

"Why don't you join us for lunch?" he asked.

A second invitation for a meal with him and another woman. Why did he feel obliged to include her? Probably just pity. The thought rankled, but this time she was tempted. Except the last thing she needed was to watch Nick, up close and personal, being nice to his mom. She read all the women's magazines. The articles said a man who was good to his mother was the best kind of husband material. Abby wasn't looking for a husband, and had no intention of becoming a wife before she'd had a chance to find the right guy for her. She had seen what happened when a relationship was rushed. Her parents had been each other's first, and they'd had to marry.

But this was first-hand confirmation that the articles were right about him being irresistible. There was nothing sweeter or more appealing than a guy who took his mother to lunch and was actually looking forward to it.

She shook her head. "Thanks for the offer, but I can't." Before he forced her to come up with a phony excuse she said, "So, are you going to tell me why you dropped in?"

"Actually I needed to talk to Rebecca about something."

Her manager. So, he hadn't come to see her at all. She stifled her momentary pang of disappointment. She told herself that it truly was for the best that he didn't want her. If she said it enough, she might actually believe it.

"I'm sorry, Nick. She's not here."

He frowned. "I thought she was coming in a couple of days a week to get back in the groove."

"She is. But mother and baby had a bad night. She's coming in tomorrow. Shall I try her at home?" she asked, gripping the phone. It was still warm from his touch.

Nick shook his head. "Don't bother her. It can wait. I'll call her tomorrow."

"I'll let her know you stopped by," she offered.

"Thanks, Ab. I'm sorry I don't have time right now to discuss your ideas." He looked at his watch and shook his head. "But drop by my office and we can talk."

"Okay."

He snapped his fingers. "Any day but Thursday. I've got meetings all day."

"Okay."

"See you soon." He smiled, a look that would make ice a goner. Then he was gone.

She really wanted to discuss her plans with Nick. The last time had been exhilarating. She'd never known work could be so much fun. But every time she saw him, Abby had more and more trouble recovering her professional detachment. She hadn't worked her tail off just to watch her career fall apart because of one slip on a Twister mat. A slip that had made her aware of him in ways she'd never been before. Maybe if they'd actually kissed, she would be able to put it in perspective. And forget about it. But they hadn't, and she had to put it, and Nick, out of her mind.

If it was the last thing she ever did, she had to straighten her politically correct mask and get back on business track. She would treat him like a boss. Deferential distance. Piece of cake, she told herself. If only she believed it.

Thursday afternoon, Nick cancelled all his meetings after receiving a phone call from his mother. He headed for his brother Joe's office to tell him about the conversation and started to push open the door when he heard a woman's voice.

"Thanks, Joe. I needed that." Abby?

Why was she in his brother's office? More important, what had Joe given her that she needed? Maybe most important, why had those simple words tied him in knots?

"You're welcome," Joe said. "Don't worry, Abby. It'll get easier."

What? Nick's irritation clicked up a notch. Abby had promised to come and see him. Why was she there on the day he'd told her he would be tied up? What was she doing with his brother? The restaurant where she worked was only a few miles from the corporate office so it was reasonable for her to drop in any time.

"I don't know if it will get easier, but thanks for listening," she said.

"I'm always available. Come here."

Not only was eavesdropping slimy and underhanded, it didn't set well with a man of action. Nick walked through the doorway. The knot in his gut tightened when he saw Joe holding Abby. His brother was a big man, as tall as Nick. She seemed to disappear in his arms. Nick hadn't felt like this since his wife had dumped him for her old boyfriend. He'd done his best to keep the feelings from ever kicking up again. But here they were. Because of his brother. And Abby.

Joe was a people person, a good thing since he was the Director of Human Resources for Marchetti's Inc. He looked over Abby's blond head and smiled. "Hey, Nick."

Abby glanced at him. "Nick!" Quickly she stepped away from his brother.

Nick didn't miss her guilty look or the pink in her cheeks. "Hi, Abby."

He studied Joe. Nothing out of the ordinary there, but his brother had had a lot of experience with women. Abby had none with men. If Joe decided to put the moves on her, she hadn't acquired the know-how to deal with the situation. But Joe wouldn't take advantage of that. Would he?

Joe's grin faded. "You look as if you'd like to yank the head off a doll. What's up?"

"That's what I'd like to know."

Abby tucked her hair behind her ear. "Is something wrong?"

Nick met her gaze. "You tell me."

Tell me what you're doing here with my brother when I specifically told you I was unavailable today.

Nick realized a couple of things in one of those moments of crystal clarity. He didn't want Abby alone with playboy, confirmed bachelor, charming, outgoing Joe Marchetti. His second thought was that no way did he want another man hugging Abby, not even his own brother, especially his irresistible brother. His third was that he had no right to entertain thoughts number one and two. Unfortunately, that was the world's smallest thought and didn't diminish his testosterone surge one bit. Apparently his protective instinct for Abby was on overdrive. What else could it be?

He cleared his throat as he tried to get a grip on his anger. "What are you doing here?"

Abby glanced up at his brother, another quick, guilty look. "Rebecca looked over the quarterly report and was worried about the numbers. We discussed some of my ideas, and she agreed that they could generate business at the restaurant. She sent me over here."

Nick's feelings took a detour into something territorial. She had first broached that subject with *him.*

Joe rested a hip on his desk and folded his arms over his chest. "She's got some dynamite plans, Nick. Two-for-one coupons, poor-but-hungry Tuesday, and—"

"All-you-can-eat family night," Nick finished.

Joe nodded enthusiastically. "Yeah. So she talked to you about this."

"Some," he answered.

Abby looked at him, worry creasing her forehead. "You were in a meeting, Nick. I was looking for Luke to run the numbers by him, but he's not around. Joe saw me in the hall and called me in. He was kind enough to listen to everything, including my whining."

Nick couldn't erase his mental picture of Abby in his brother's arms. "So what was the hug for?" he snapped.

"Just company T.L.C. Abby isn't used to being a

manager," Joe said. "She doesn't like calling off employees."

Nick knew he was being a jerk, but couldn't seem to help it. "Is that right?"

"Absolutely." Joe had that I-know-something-you-don't-know look on his face.

Nick didn't like it any better now than he had when they were kids. "Well you're wrong. It doesn't get easier."

Nick hadn't felt this irrational since that summer he'd spent in Phoenix. But there was no connection between what happened then and Abby. She was his friend. He hated it when rational thought returned. The bad part of a testosterone surge was picking up the pieces after he'd shot off his mouth. How could he salvage the situation?

There was only one intelligent choice—make a stupid excuse for his churlish behavior and look like a jackass for a few seconds. It was the course of action better known as Plan B, or retreat and run like hell. He didn't want to think about the way seeing Abby with his brother had made him feel. He decided it was just a fluke. His one foray into a relationship and the disaster that followed had destroyed the part of him that rationally processed relationship information.

He ran a hand through his hair. "Sorry, Joe. Rough morning."

"I thought you were in meetings."

"I cancelled them. Just got a call from Ma. Grandma is in the hospital having tests."

"Yeah, your secretary gave me the message." Worry creased his brother's forehead. "Does Dad know? He was supposed to play golf today."

"He's there with them. So is Luke." He looked at

Abby. "That's why you couldn't find him. Alex is out of town, but I left a message with his secretary."

"What's wrong with your grandmother?" Abby asked, obviously concerned.

"Chest pain," Nick answered.

"I'm so sorry," Abby said. "Is there anything I can do?"

"Thanks, but no. Actually I was on my way there when I saw you," Joe said.

"Why didn't you tell me?" she cried. "This could have waited. Don't let me stop you. Go." Abby linked her arm through Joe's and tugged him forward.

For Nick, that playful, familiar touch was like a hot wind over glowing sparks. White-hot flames licked through him. He was beginning to see a pattern here. But something else bothered him more. Even if it was Luke she wanted to see, she'd deliberately dropped by on a day he, Nick, had told her he was unavailable. Why?

The obvious answer was that she was avoiding him. Something had changed between them, and Nick didn't like it. He wanted back the comfortable camaraderie. Which made him glad his mother had given him a mission.

"I'm on my way," Joe said, heading for the door.

Nick decided turnabout was fair play. If Joe planned to dish it out, he'd best be prepared to take it. "Last time I checked the hospital, obstetrics and cardiology were nowhere near each other."

"What's that supposed to mean?" Joe asked good-naturedly.

That was Nick's least favorite thing about his brother. Joe was annoyingly cheerful most of the time. Getting to him was a challenge. "You're surprisingly eager to go to the hospital. You wouldn't by any chance be planning to stop by the O.B. department and harass that nurse you met when Rosie had her baby?"

Joe folded his arms over his chest and grinned. "Absolutely not."

Nick shook his head. "Go see what's up with the family."

Joe gave him a mock salute. "I hear and obey, fearless leader. Do you want me to wait for you?"

Nick shook his head. "I need my car. I'll be a couple minutes behind you."

"Okay," Joe said. He looked at Abby. "I like your ideas. In fact, you deserve a bonus. But I'm in charge of personnel, not number-crunching." He winked at her and angled his head toward Nick. "Talk to Mr. Congeniality about the dough."

Abby figured this was a bad time to talk about a raise when Nick looked like a volcano about to erupt. In all the years she'd known him, she'd seen him happy and carefree. She'd seen him angry and upset. But she had never seen him look the way he had after she'd hugged his brother. Next to Nick, Joe Marchetti was the closest thing she had to her own big brother.

Which was why she'd decided to approach Luke when she knew Nick was occupied. A good decision, since it was awfully difficult to keep her mind on her work when he stood there looking like a model. He was wearing charcoal pants and a crisp, long-sleeved white shirt. The sleeves were rolled up, indicating that he'd been working. The corded muscles in his forearms were dusted with dark hair and so powerful, he could as easily have been a construction worker as a business executive.

His tie was slightly loosened, just enough so that he

was comfortable, but he could quickly have it back in place if necessary. The pattern on the silk was like an Impressionist painting in blue, green, mauve and a whole lot of other colors.

"I like your tie," she said. After the words popped out, she wanted to smack her forehead and call them back. Way too forward. She shouldn't notice what he was wearing. Correction—she couldn't help but notice. But she was just this side of horrified that the comment had slipped from her lips so easily.

Absently, he looked down at his tie. "Thanks. Madison gave me this."

No doubt it was expensive. And intimate. Not as much as boxer shorts with big red hearts, but definitely something Abby would never in a million years be in a position to give him. Time to steer the conversation in a different direction. Or better yet, leave so he could be with his family.

"I'm sorry. This obviously isn't a good time. You need to get to the hospital. I'll go—"

"Don't." He sighed as he passed her and sat on the corner of Joe's desk. "Not yet."

He looked upset, and Abby had the most absurd desire to put her arms around him and comfort him. As much as she wanted to escape from him, and her budding attraction to him, she couldn't walk out. She had the feeling he needed to talk. "You're very fond of your grandmother, aren't you?"

He nodded. "We all are. But Luke is her favorite."

"How come? You're the oldest," she said. "You came first."

He shrugged. "Yeah. But there's a special bond between her and Luke."

"I never knew my grandparents."

"None of them?"

She shook her head. "They lived in another state. We never visited. Then one by one, they were all gone."

"That's too bad. It's a special relationship, and a responsibility."

There he was, being Mr. Wonderful again. She needed to get out because of how very much she wanted to stay, because she very much enjoyed talking to him. She looked at the watch on her wrist. Although she knew the play smacked of *golly, look at the time*, it was the best exit line she could come up with. "Golly, look at the time. I've really got to get back to work. And you have to go—"

"Wait, Ab."

"We can talk work another time."

"No, it's something else." He folded his arms over his chest. "While we were at lunch the other day, Mom asked me to invite you and Sarah to Thanksgiving dinner."

"She did? Why?"

"Your name came up, and Ma wondered if you'd like to join us."

"Why did my name come up?"

"Let's just say that the salmon wasn't the only thing being grilled," he said wryly. "So what do you say?"

After her shock wore off, so many things rushed through Abby's mind. First, why had he and his mother been talking about her? Thought number two was overwhelming gratitude that she and Sarah wouldn't be alone for another holiday.

Unfortunately, thought number three was the brain cycle where she started thinking the situation to death. Why was he asking? He could have told his mother the invitation was inappropriate. But he hadn't. This overstepped the boss/employee boundary. Worse—she was afraid he felt sorry for her. She hated that.

She was quiet for so long, Nick finally asked, "Do you have other plans?"

"No," she answered quickly, honestly. Then she could have bitten her tongue. Everything else she thought to death. Not this time. He had given her the perfect out if only she'd kept her mouth shut two seconds longer. Where was the world's biggest roll of duct tape when she really needed it?

He nodded with satisfaction. "Good, then I'll tell Ma to expect two more."

"I didn't say that."

He frowned. "So I'll tell Ma you would rather be alone than have dinner with us?"

"Don't you dare," she said. "That's not what I said."

"That's what I heard."

"Then you should have your hearing checked." She winced when she realized what she'd said. The last time she was alone with him she'd called him names, now she was insulting him again. She took a deep breath. "I didn't mean that. Exactly."

"I know. Do you want to tell me what you do mean—exactly?"

Two could play at answering a question with a question. "What would Madison say about having us there?"

"She doesn't get a vote."

That shouldn't have made Abby happy. But doggone it, inside she was doing the dance of joy. "How come?"

"Madison and I are taking a break from each other. I thought I already told you."

"You said there was a dialogue. I didn't know it was a done deal." Abby was stunned. If he kept dropping bombshells, she was going to wind up in cardiology having tests, too. He'd hinted about this that day in her office, but he hadn't come right out and said they were kaput. "Was it mutual?"

"It was her idea."

"Nick, I'm sorry." She really was. After the drubbing he'd taken from the woman he'd married, this must be like salt in the wound. "Just remember, what doesn't kill you will make you stronger. You got through it once, you're a pro now. I know I teased you about Madison not being right for you, but I never wished for you to be hurt. The two of you will work it out."

"I'm fine, Abby."

"Really?"

"Yeah, really. But my mother is fond of Madison. She's taking it hard."

"Tell me this isn't the reason my name came up at lunch," she begged.

"Okay, consider yourself told."

Abby didn't believe him for a minute. How could she be to blame for the breakup? There was nothing between her and Nick except a work relationship. "I don't know what to say."

"She'll get over it. Look, say you'll come to Thanksgiving. You already admitted you don't have other plans. Ma will be hurt if you turn her down."

She hoped that was the truth because it would mean that Mrs. Marchetti didn't blame her for what had happened between Madison and her son.

"She really wants us there?"

"If she didn't, she wouldn't have extended the invitation. You haven't lived until you've experienced a Marchetti holiday."

"What about your grandmother?"

"We're going to keep our fingers crossed that this is nothing serious. If the worst happens, we'll go with Plan B. Until then, we'll assume that it's business as usual. And I would very much like you to be there."

Abby felt like she was standing on a cliff, one foot solid on the ground, the other poised in the air. She could pull back, or free-fall. It would have been safe if he was still involved with Madison. Although, he'd said breaking it off was Madison's idea. So he still had feelings for her. Which meant that as far as she, Abby, was concerned, it was still harmless. And with the rest of his family there, she would barely see him. But his last words tipped the scale.

"So what do you say? Will you come?"

She took a deep breath, then smiled. "Yes."

Chapter Six

Florence Marchetti graciously held court at the head of the table while her husband, Tom, charmed everyone at his end. Abby watched, feeling as if she was dreaming the best holiday she'd ever had. The day had been magical so far. All the Marchettis had treated the Ridgeway sisters as part of the family from the moment they'd arrived. Nick had teased and joked, behaving like the friend he'd always been to her. She was finally relaxing into the spirit of the festivities.

Flo glanced at each member of her family, then smiled warmly at her two guests. "Gentlemen, and ladies, this is the portion of the program where everyone has to tell what he—or she—is thankful for."

"All together now," Nick said. In unison with his siblings, he groaned loudly.

Abby couldn't help laughing. She was sitting, to Mrs. M.'s right, tucked between Joe and Luke with Grandma on her left. Sarah sat beside the older woman and directly across from Alex. Nick was on one side of his dad, and his sister Rosie with her husband Steve and six-month-old baby Stephanie on the other. The flowers, silverware, matching crystal and china were breathtaking on the Italian lace tablecloth.

Abby couldn't believe she was a guest. She was still shaking her head over the fact that eleven adults and one baby in a high chair were comfortably seated at this feast. There wasn't a folding table or chair in sight. And she, Abby, was included.

This must be the equivalent of the fairy-tale ball. But Abby would bet her gravy and mashed potatoes that no one made Cinderella give a speech about how grateful she was. So every fairy tale had a price. Soon it would be Abby's turn to come up with something articulate and witty—all the Marchettis were glib and interesting—and actually speak about what she was thankful for. Unless a miracle or a disaster happened, she didn't have a snowball's chance in hell of getting out of it.

From the opposite end of the table, Tom Marchetti said, "You start, Flo."

"Thank you, dear. I'm grateful for my healthy family." The woman's glowing gaze lingered on her granddaughter, then moved on and stopped at her mother-in-law. "I'm thankful that Grandma's tests showed she had nothing more than high gas pains. And I'm very, very thankful that Sarah and Abby could join us today to equalize the male-to-female ratio."

"Amen to that," Rosie said. "Steve and I have done our part with a baby girl. But the rest of you are lagging." She glanced lovingly at her husband, then sternly looked at her four older brothers. "What's the holdup, guys?"

"No holdup," Luke explained. "That would imply

a delay in a plan to have children. Hard to do when you're a confirmed bachelor like myself and my brothers." He looked around. "Right, guys?"

Joe nodded agreement. "That means we're never getting married," he clarified. "But if I do, and that's a very big *if*, I will produce only male children."

"Like you have so much control," Rosie teased.

"Don't go there, sis," Joe said. "You'll lose that argument."

"I know who determines the sex of the baby," Rosie scoffed. "I was talking about the 'married' part."

Joe shot her a disbelieving look. "You don't think I can fend off a determined woman bent on marriage?"

Rosie laughed. "I think you'll fall like a ton of bricks when you meet the right woman, so don't even talk to me about controlling a romantic situation."

Abby breathed a sigh of relief that their verbal sparring gave her a reprieve from the thanks-giving speeches. On top of that, it gave her an opportunity to observe all the Marchetti men in one place and in action. She studied Nick, who was putting away a fair amount of turkey and dressing. He was the best-looking by far, she decided, among an impressive display of masculinity. Joe and Alex had the same dark coloring. Luke's hair was lighter brown and he was the only one with blue eyes. She had never noticed that before.

"Marchetti men have control over everything, at all times," Alex said. "Including marriage."

"Right on, bro. That said," Joe continued, "I guess I'm thankful that I'm not married."

"Don't knock it till you've tried it." Rosie's husband, Steve Schafer, gestured with his fork. His dark-blond hair and blue-eyed good looks were an attractive counterpoint to his wife's wildly curly black hair and brown eyes.

"Rosie told you to say that," Alex said.

"I did not." She shot him a glare, then leaned down to retrieve the rattle her daughter had dropped.

"She didn't," Steve agreed. "Marrying Rosie and having the baby were the best things that ever happened to me."

"She's the most beautiful baby in the whole world," Sarah chimed in.

"Stephanie is the best," Joe agreed. "Too bad you were also forced to take my sister in the merger."

"I'd be a mess without Rosie," Steve said with heartfelt sincerity. The look he gave his wife was filled with so much love, Abby felt it clear down at her end of the table.

"Thank you, honey." Rosie leaned over and kissed her husband's lean cheek. "I suppose it's no secret that I've loved you since I was a girl. As far as I'm concerned, you still walk on water."

Abby suddenly realized what the phrase "lonely in a crowd" meant. And the term "third wheel." Seeing this young couple so much in love opened an ache inside her. Would she ever find something like that? Absolutely, came her answer. Just as soon as she had the time to look.

"It's gettin' deep in here," Joe said.

"You can say that again," Alex agreed.

"I third that," Luke chimed in. "You're awfully quiet, Nick. Does this mean you're weakening on the subject of marriage? Is there going to be an announcement soon about you and Madison?"

Nick met Abby's gaze down the expanse of table.

"No. She broke it off. She thinks I have feelings for Abby."

Abby felt eleven pairs of eyes on her. It would have been twelve, but baby Stephanie was busy examining her fingers. A ten-second thankful speech would have been easier.

"Nick mentioned that to me," Flo said. "And I've found Madison to be quite perceptive."

"She's wrong this time," Abby answered. She remembered Nick saying that his mother liked Madison and was disappointed about the rift. "Besides, I think they'll work it out. They're just taking a break from each other."

"Interesting," Luke said. "She's beautiful and brainy, with a body that—"

"Careful, Luke," his mother warned. "We have an impressionable teenage girl here."

"Thanks, Mrs. M.," Sarah said. "But I've heard worse. High-school guys are so gross."

"What about Austin?" Nick asked her.

"He's different," Sarah answered, looking down at her plate as a blush crept into her cheeks.

"We're getting off the subject," Luke said. "Whose idea was it to take a break?" he asked Nick.

The edge in his voice drew Abby's attention to him and the way he stared at his older brother. Something had kicked up the intensity in his already intense blue eyes. Interesting, she thought.

"It was hers," Nick answered.

"Then she had her reasons," Tom Marchetti interjected.

"Getting back to what we're thankful for," Nick said, changing the subject again. "I'm more thankful than I can say that I'm not married."

"Me too," Joe said.

"Me three," Alex added.

"Never have, never will," Luke chimed in fervently.

Flo Marchetti looked around the table, clearly puzzled by her sons' attitude. She fixed her gaze on Nick. "*You're* responsible for this."

"Me? What did I do?"

"You're the oldest. The leader of the pack. You set the pace. You've obviously done something, or said something, to turn your brothers off to the institution of marriage."

"That's ridiculous, Ma." Nick's eyes sparkled with humor.

"Don't blame Nick," Joe said. Abby liked the way he jumped to his brother's defense. "We're not a pack of sheep." He glared at Rosie when she made a *baa* sound, then continued. "We don't follow the leader. We can think for ourselves."

"Darn right we can," Nick seconded.

"You know, Flo," Tom Marchetti interjected, "it's really none of our business. When the boys are ready and the time is right, they'll get married. You can't rush these things."

The woman smiled at her husband. "You're right, dear. But I can't help being a little impatient at the amount of time they're taking. I'm not getting any younger. I would like more grandchildren. And this attitude. What makes you all so positive that marriage is something to be strenuously avoided?" Flo looked around her table at each of her sons. "There's a saying—"

"Never judge anyone till you've walked a mile in his sneakers," Nick, Joe, Alex, Luke and Rosie all chimed in together.

"Apparently I've said that once or twice before. And I thought no one listened to me." Flo grinned at their good-natured teasing. "Except for Rosie and Steve, none of your sneakers has ever walked down the aisle. So how can you be so sure marriage is the pits?"

"It clips a man's wings." Joe shrugged.

"Have you ever been married?" she shot back.

"Of course not, but—"

"Then don't talk to me." She looked at Alex and Luke in turn. "You two?"

"No, but—"

"Then you don't get an opinion." She fixed Nick with a look that even a covert operative trained to resist terrorist interrogation would have trouble ignoring. "Nick?"

Abby was puzzled. Surely they knew about Nick's marriage. Why would his mother dwell on something that had hurt her son so badly?

As his silence stretched, Flo Marchetti's eyes narrowed on the son in question. "You have that look, Nick."

The eldest of the macho Marchetti brothers squirmed. "What look? I don't have a look."

"Since you were a little boy, and you did something you were ashamed of, you would get an expression on your face."

"You're imagining things, Ma," he said shrugging.

Flo shook her head. "I can't explain it. Just something a mother knows. So I say again, how can you judge the institution of marriage when you've never been married?"

Nick met his mother's gaze, then glanced quickly at his father who was watching him intently. He looked at Abby, then said, "I suppose it's about time you knew. I *was* married."

It was as if the cone of silence had descended over the table. No one said a word; all of them stared at Nick. Abby could tell from the genuine expressions of shock that no one in his family had known about this. She didn't know what to make of the fact that he'd told *her*. Good heavens. Why?

The stunned, unnatural quiet stretched on and grew awkward. Finally, Flo cleared her throat. When she spoke, her voice was surprisingly soft. "Why didn't you tell us, Nick?"

"It's not something I'm proud of. Like you said, I'm the oldest. I set the pace. Some standard, huh?"

"But we're your family, son." His father's gaze held sympathy.

Nick is hating this, Abby thought, studying his smoldering eyes and tight jaw.

Thoughtfully, his mother took a sip of wine. "It happened that summer you worked in Phoenix."

Nick nodded. "She was pregnant." There was a gasp of surprise from Rosie.

"With your baby?" Tom Marchetti's tone was controlled, barely.

"No. The father walked out on her. I cared about her, so I proposed. I wanted to take care of her and the baby. She said yes."

"So what happened?" Joe looked shell-shocked.

"The jerk came back. He had a change of heart."

"And so did the woman?" Flo's expression was angry, a mother lioness protecting her cub.

Abby knew exactly how she felt. She saw the miserable look in Nick's eyes and wanted to wrap her arms around him. At the same time, she would give anything to have five minutes alone with the witch who had made him look like that. There would be a tongue-lashing of monumental proportions.

Nick heaved a sigh. "Yeah, she took him back. Said she loved him and it would be best for him to raise his child. She got an annulment."

"Why didn't you tell us?" Rosie asked, shock and indignation in her voice. "I don't understand how you could keep something like this a secret from your family."

That makes two of us, Abby thought.

"Yeah." Steve's face, normally impassive, showed his confusion and hurt. "You never said a word."

Nick ran a hand through his hair. "It was a stupid thing to do. Not one of my better moments. I didn't think it was necessary to share my humiliation."

It wasn't that, Abby thought. And he wasn't a coward. He'd been terribly used. She glanced around the table and saw the same expression in everyone's eyes—pain and anger. He hadn't wanted his family to suffer, too. The need to shield them had kept him quiet. But he also felt it was his mistake to fix. All alone. How awful for him, she realized. Keeping the feelings bottled up inside him. Again, she had the urge to wrap her arms around him and comfort him.

"Well no wonder you're a confirmed bachelor," Luke said. "The woman in Phoenix, then Madison. You're zero for two, bro."

There was a teasing note in his voice, but Abby sensed it was too soon for one of Nick's wry grins. She knew her instinct was right when Nick glared at his brother and stood up. "I think I'll get some air. Just talk amongst yourselves."

* * *

Standing on the sidewalk outside his parents' home, Nick dragged in a breath of air. It was dusk, and a stiff breeze made the November evening chilly. Not to mention the hovering moisture that hinted of rain. But after being on the family hot seat, it felt pretty good. So the cat was finally out of the bag. He felt two parts relief mixed with a dash of embarrassment and anger. Which wasn't nearly as bad as he'd expected.

Somehow, telling Abby first had taken a lot of the sting from the wound. He had to thank her again for that.

The front door opened. He didn't look around to see who it was. Either his mother or sister, he suspected. They'd both want to give him a shoulder to cry on.

Amazingly, he found he didn't need to cry. He'd come outside because he didn't want to talk about it anymore, and he knew they needed to.

A single set of footsteps sounded behind him on the concrete. Then a familiar fragrance surrounded him. Abby. His gut tightened with anticipation, and his nerve endings began to tingle. His heart rate kicked up. His powerful physical response to her worried him. He had just come clean about his one and only folly. He'd vowed never to take a chance again. No way did he want a repeat performance.

Standing beside him, Abby faced into the chill wind. It blew the hair off her face. She was wearing black slacks and a fuzzy, soft-looking royal-blue sweater that he'd noticed earlier made her eyes sparkle like rare and beautiful sapphires.

"You never told your family, Nick." She spoke softly, but her tone was filled with censure.

"It would only have hurt them, and there was nothing they could have done."

"I know that."

"I'm the golden boy. I got dumped in a big way. I didn't want their pity."

"I figured that, too."

Since when had she gotten to know him so well? He looked down at her pensive profile as she stood beside him. "My humiliation is complete. I finally told them."

She glanced at him, then started to pace back and forth in front of him on the sidewalk. "You have nothing to feel sorry about. That woman gets the blue ribbon for dumb. She hurt a great guy like you. There should be a special place in hell for her. You were willing to be a father to her baby, and she tossed you aside like yesterday's linguine for the jerk who hadn't the decency to marry her right away." She walked four paces, then stomped back and stared indignantly up at him.

Nick was stunned. When he'd first told her, she'd been supportive and bracing. And he liked that. He also liked that somewhere in her passionate monologue there was rage on his behalf. On top of everything else, he couldn't help thinking that she was beautiful when she was angry.

And he wanted to kiss her.

Big mistake, he told himself. Don't go there.

She continued to walk back and forth, shaking her head and mumbling. He could almost see the steam coming out of her ears. A smart man didn't step in front of an out-of-control locomotive. Nick considered himself to have above-average intelligence. He folded his arms over his chest and watched for several moments in surprised fascination.

Finally he couldn't stand the suspense and had to ask, "Why are you so mad now?" he asked.

"Because I saw what it did to you, telling them like that." She stopped in front of him and put her hand on his arm.

"Thanks to you, it wasn't as bad as I'd thought."

In fact, she made a lot of things better. Except his sleep. Ever since the night he'd almost kissed her, he couldn't seem to get the thought out of his mind. How would she feel? What would she taste of? Would she kiss him back with all the passion he suspected simmered below her cool, controlled surface? Did she wonder about kissing him, too?

He couldn't help hoping she did. But as far as he was concerned, his imagination was the only part of him that would know.

"Why thanks to me?" Abby stared up at him, then stepped back.

"For listening when I needed to talk."

Anger mixed with a healthy dose of fear in her eyes. "Don't try to distract me when I'm mad at you, Nick Marchetti."

"Me? What did I do?"

"It's what you *didn't* do," she said hotly. "Why in the world would you keep something as important as getting married from your family? And your best friend," she added, frowning at him.

"Wait a minute, Ab—"

"No, you wait. What's up with that, Nick? They care about you. They had every right to know. It's what families are all about. They stand by each other."

"And take care of each other. That's what I did—protect them."

"One of the things I miss most about my folks is not having someone to go to when bad stuff happens."

"You've got me, pal. Dial M for—" He stopped when she glared at him.

"You're lucky enough to have a mother and father, four brothers and a sister, and you robbed them of the opportunity to be there for you."

"There was nothing they could have done, and I wanted to spare them the pain as I've told you."

"So you hid it. And made them think you're a selfish bastard who's soured on marriage for no apparent reason."

"I didn't aggressively hide anything. I simply chose not to share any of those details with them. Do you blame me?"

"Yes." She shivered and folded her arms over her chest, in a self-protective gesture. "What's her name?" she asked suddenly.

He shook his head, trying to follow her thought process. Giving up, he asked, "Who?"

"Your ex-wife. You never told me her name."

He let out a long breath. "Margaret."

Saying her name out loud after all this time brought back a barrage of images. Black hair and eyes, a volatile temper he'd mistaken for passion. He remembered what it cost him to bury the pain.

He clenched his jaw, then finally looked at her and said, "I gave her everything, Ab, and it wasn't enough. I know you disagree and this will sound weird, but divorce would almost have been better than an annulment."

She didn't touch him except with her gaze, but he felt the caress. "I hate her for what she did to you,

Nick. And something else. She robbed you of letting your family share the pain with you."

But Nick had always felt it was his punishment, his own private suffering, his to do with as he pleased. It pleased him to keep the pain from his family. And for reasons he still didn't know or understand, it had pleased him to share the secret with Abby. His friend. Someone who could understand. Considering that, her response seemed out of whack.

"What's really upsetting you, Ab?"

"I told you. Keeping this to yourself is selfish—"

He shook his head. "It's more than that. There's something else eating you."

"What makes you say that?"

"Because you're acting strange. As if this is personal. As far as I know, I haven't done anything except share something from my past with you. I could be wrong, but most people would consider that a compliment. So out with it. What's wrong?"

"You kept this secret for a long time. Not a word or a hint to the people closest to you."

"And?"

She looked up. "You had no right to tell me first."

Chapter Seven

"No right? Tell you first? What does that mean?"

"You're brighter than the average bear, Nick. Figure it out."

Abby couldn't believe she'd blurted that out. She *was* angry, and surprised that he'd figured out so effortlessly that it was personal. Confiding a secret of that magnitude implied a bond between them. That was dangerous territory. But she'd never intended to tell him. More than anything she wished she could call the words back. How had she messed up so badly?

But she knew. One minute she was pacing, the next she stopped and looked at him. Something in his expression had told her he wanted to kiss her. That's when she'd stepped back and the words popped out.

It was scary and wonderful all at the same time. All of her feminine responses kicked in, apparently at the expense of her brain function. The line between friendship, a working relationship and something even more serious was so blurred she wasn't sure she could find it, let alone walk it any more. Now what was she going to do?

Nothing.

"C'mon, Abby. You can't say something like that and not explain what you meant."

"Don't you see, Nick? I don't want to be your third strike."

He looked at her as if she had two heads, then shrugged. "What's baseball got to do with this? You've really lost me this time."

Abby wanted to run far and fast. Then maybe she really could lose him. Because more than anything she wanted him to kiss her. Her heart was telling her one thing, and she had to tell him something else. Because if he ever did kiss her, she didn't have the will to stop him. And if she didn't stop him, there would be hell to pay. But he was right. She owed him an explanation.

"It's like Luke said. Margaret, then Madison. You're zero for two. I don't want to be number three."

"Look on the bright side. At least your name doesn't start with M."

"Don't joke about this. I'm serious."

"Okay. Just what are you so serious about?"

She threw up her hands. "I can't believe I have to spell it out for you."

"Sorry. I guess the alphabet is a weak area for me. What's got you so upset?"

"Telling me this secret before breathing a word to your family implies an intimacy to our relationship."

He scratched his head. "I'm still lost."

The wind blew and she shivered. Amazing, she'd been so *hot* just a few moments ago.

Nick pulled her into his arms. "You're going to catch your death."

"We should go inside." She put up a token resistance, but sighed and stopped when he didn't release her.

"Not so fast, pal. We need to talk about this and something tells me you don't want to do that in front of the meddling Marchettis. I love them all, but—"

"You're right."

Craving his warmth and security, she let herself snuggle against him. What could it hurt? She couldn't imagine repeating this experience ever again. And maybe *he* needed a hug. She certainly hadn't had enough in the last five years. It felt wonderful, like coming home, but to no home she'd ever known. She'd never felt so safe before.

"So talk, Ab."

"Okay," she said. "Here's the way I see it. Bombshells like you just dropped in there—when everyone was supposed to be saying what they're thankful for, I might add—usually happen in a very specific order. You usually lay it on someone you're close to first."

"I did that. You're my friend."

"True. But it should have been your mother."

"No way. There's nowhere Margaret would have been safe from the wrath of Florence Evelyn Marchetti. And remember, she was pregnant."

"This is nothing to joke about, Nick."

"Who's joking? My mother would have taken her apart." But with her cheek against his chest, Abby felt as well as heard him chuckle.

"Okay then, your best *guy* friend, or your sister or brother—and you have three to choose from, for goodness' sake. Someone other than me."

"What's wrong with you?"

"Where do I start?" She sighed. "Nowhere. Because I'm not going to let you turn this around and make it about me. Trauma is a step-by-step process. You took a giant leap over your support system and came to me. I'm concerned that you have unrealistic expectations.''

"So?" He looked down at her. "I'm not saying you're right about this. I just want to understand where you're going.''

"Nowhere. That's my point. I don't have time for a relationship. I don't want to have one. But most of all, I don't want you to get hurt.''

"Strike three?" The tone of his voice told her that he was finding this very entertaining.

"Exactly. And please stop laughing at me.''

"Heaven forbid.'' He snuggled her closer, and God help her, she let him. God help her again, she enjoyed it.

"For the sake of argument," he continued, resting his chin on the top of her head, "let's just say I had feelings for you—''

"Don't do this, Nick," she warned.

"What?" he asked, sounding as innocent as a choir-boy.

Maneuvering Marchetti was at it again, she thought. "I owe you more than I can ever repay. I don't want to jeopardize our very special association.''

"Define jeopardy.''

"Margaret and Madison.'' It was hard, but she made herself leave the safety of his arms. "I work for you. But more than that, I don't want you to get hurt ever again.''

"How do you know that would happen?''

"For starters, I don't have what it takes to do the relationship thing right now.''

"And what does it take?"

"Time." She looked at him. "Besides, I may be way off base. Feel free to tell me my imagination is running away with me. At any moment you can stop me and say that you tell perfect strangers your deepest, darkest secrets on an alarmingly regular basis."

He stuck his hands in his jeans pockets and shook his head. "Can't say that I do."

"Okay, then let me remind you of something that apparently has slipped your mind. Things are not over with Madison. A fact I felt compelled to mention to your brother Luke before I came outside. He didn't seem too pleased about the fact that you and Madison are going to get back together." She took a breath. "But there's every chance you'll work things out with her."

"Not likely."

"She's a good person, Nick. You could do worse."

"And in fact I did," he said.

"Are you taking this at all seriously?"

"Of course. But you're missing the point. The fact that I can joke about the past is a sign that it's no longer painful for me. In an odd sort of way, telling you, saying it out loud, made it go away. It was kind of a dress rehearsal for telling the family, and that made it much easier. I'm very serious when I say that you had a lot to do with that, my friend. Thank you."

Just a few moments ago he'd said that to her, right after he'd almost kissed her. Would he finally do it? Her chest tightened with anticipation and need that twisted into a painful ache. "Me? How?" she asked, her voice breathless.

"You listened. You were on my side." He folded his arms over his chest. "You said all the right things.

I didn't feel so damn stupid anymore. It was like holding your breath when you know something will hurt like hell. I've been doing that for a long time. I finally let myself feel it, and found out it hasn't got the bite anymore."

"I'm glad I could help. But that doesn't change anything. I want to clarify the situation between us once and for all. I'm not ready for a one-on-one, exclusive dating thing. I look forward to that eventually. But I found out the hard way that waiting doesn't work."

"Relax, Ab. One of the things I like best about you is your honesty. And friendship. That's why I confided in you. No one said anything about dating."

"Really?"

Nick wanted to say more. But the look in her eyes stopped him. Abby was right. There was something going on between them, or he never would have told her about Margaret. And she would deny it, but he would bet that the blazing look in her eyes meant that she wanted him to kiss her. But he would be six kinds of fool to pursue a relationship with someone so vehemently opposed to it.

Because he'd fallen hard and fast for Margaret, he'd taken a chance with her, a woman who had compelling reasons to make it work. The whole affair had been an unmitigated disaster. He wasn't anxious to repeat a mistake of that magnitude. Besides, love didn't sneak up on him. It hit him suddenly, and right between the eyes. Until that happened, he'd remain a confirmed bachelor.

"Really. I don't want anything serious any more than you do. We're good friends, nothing more. To friendship," he said, holding out his hand.

She smiled as she put her cold fingers in his palm.

"I'm glad you understand. I don't ever want to lose what we have."

Her hand was freezing. "Then I suggest we go inside before we both turn into ice sculptures."

"Before we do, there's something I need to thank you for."

Would she thank him with a kiss, the way he'd wanted to thank her just a while ago? The thought sneaked in before he could stop it. Unfortunately it got his heart rate up right along with his anticipation. "What's that?"

"Your impromptu revelation saved me from having to make a thanks-giving speech in front of your family."

"Happy to oblige," he said, looking up at the sky as he struggled to get a grip on his runaway libido. "And let me be of assistance again and get you in the house. It's starting to rain."

If he didn't put some distance between himself and Abby, getting a little wet wasn't the worst thing that could happen.

Abby let Nick lead her back inside, but she removed her hand when they reentered the dining room. She didn't want to give his family grist for gossip, especially when there was nothing to talk about. The problem was, when she and Nick stopped in the doorway, all talk abruptly ceased. Everyone stared at them. Knowing they'd been discussing his situation, she looked at Nick, waiting for him to do something.

"I'm going to say this once," he said, "then I want to drop it and finish having Thanksgiving. What happened to me in Phoenix is over. I just want to forget about it. Everyone got that?"

A general murmur of agreement went around the table.

He nodded. "Good. Finish your dinner, Abby."

"Okay," she said. No way could she actually get food past the lump in her throat, but she was mighty grateful to sit down and not be near Nick, which felt an awful lot like ground zero at the moment.

Rosie stood up and walked to her big brother, slipping her arms around his waist to hug him. "Are you really over it, Nick?"

"Yeah. Thanks, sis."

She stared up at him. "You know, big brother, what you tried to do for that ungrateful witch was very sweet. Not unlike the situation I was in. Do you ever get tired of taking care of everyone?"

He kissed the top of her head. "You're sure singing a different tune. I remember a time when you were mad about my interfering."

"Only because you carried the big brother, little sister routine too far. But you've always been my hero," she said.

The statement was followed by a series of catcalls, sighs and snorts of laughter from the various members of the Marchetti family.

"What about me?" her husband asked, feigning indignation.

"You're my knight in shining armor," Rosie said, smiling at him.

Abby envied Rosie Marchetti Schafer more than she could ever remember envying anyone. She had a wonderful husband and four doting brothers to look out for her. Not to mention a mother and father who appeared to be in the prime of their lives and devoted to each other and their offspring. Abby wondered what it would be like to have such a strong, solid support system. She almost didn't remember what it was like not to be in charge.

"Seriously, Nick," his father said, "you could have talked to us about all this."

"I know, Dad. Part of the reason I didn't was to spare you the pain of something you couldn't do anything about. The rest isn't as noble. I plain didn't want you to know how badly I screwed up."

"You?" Joe looked at him in mock surprise. "If you did, it was probably the first time in your life. Frankly, we're glad to know you're human. Next time say the word so we can rub salt in the wound while it's still fresh."

Nick laughed. "For reasons unclear to me, I actually understand that sentiment and find it comforting." He looked around the table and said, "Now can we finish dinner?"

"We're finished," his mother said. "But you and Abby haven't gotten through the first helping yet. Let me warm yours up, dear," she said reaching for Abby's plate.

"What about me, Ma?" Nick asked as he took his place beside his father.

"Cold food is nothing more than you deserve. Keeping something like that to yourself," she said, shaking her head. But Abby could see the twinkle in her eye. Knowing that the woman watched over her brood like a mother lioness, Abby realized the expression meant that she'd accepted the fact that Nick was really fine.

When they were all seated around the table again, Rosie Schafer stood. "Getting back to what we're thankful for, I've got a secret to confide, too."

Tom Marchetti shook his head. "I'm not sure my old heart can take another one."

His daughter smiled. "This one is good." She beamed at her husband and he rose, then put his arm around her waist. "We're going to have another baby."

Flo instantly went to the young couple and hugged them both. "That's wonderful. How far along are you?"

"Three months."

"How come you waited so long to spill the beans?" Joe asked.

A frown marred Rosie's brow. "The pregnancy was shaky in the beginning. I was afraid to say anything and jinx it."

"And now?" her mother asked, obviously concerned.

Rosie and Steve smiled at each other. "The doctor says there's no need for concern," he answered. He gently patted his wife's abdomen. "We're out of the woods."

One by one Rosie's brothers hugged her and shook her husband's hand. Abby noticed the longing in Nick's eyes and that Joe Marchetti was especially tender with his sister, rubbing her still-flat tummy and talking to the growing baby there. It struck her that Flo Marchetti was right. These guys wanted families, and it didn't make sense that they were still bachelors.

Abby had never laughed so much. Doing dishes had never before lifted her melancholy mood. But then, she'd never helped Flo and Rosie in the kitchen before. Nick was hanging around, directing the cleanup operation, he claimed. One by one his brothers had wandered in, then—when threatened with "woman's work"—quickly left for that football nirvana. Rosie claimed that since Sarah was keeping the baby occupied, it gave her a much-needed rest from motherhood, not that she didn't adore every minute, or almost every minute.

Nick looked at his sister as she finished putting away turkey leftovers.

"That container is awfully big, sis."

"Really?" she shot back. "If you're going to stand there and critique, maybe you would rather do this yourself?"

"No. It's just that I'm better at spatial things than you. And fridge space is finite."

"You are pompous and condescending." Rosie looked at Abby. "How do you stand him?"

"Beats the heck out of me," she answered. She found she stood him way better than she wanted to, and wished this holiday would go on forever. Or end now before she got used to how wonderful Nick and his family were.

"Hey, what happened to me being your hero?" he asked Rosie when she threw a dishtowel at him.

"You still are. I just don't want it to go to your head."

"How come I'm not your knight in shining armor?" he asked.

Rosie sighed and shook her head with exaggerated patience. "There's a specific protocol to the appointment. You need to be elevated to 'white knight' by your significant other. After that, the next step is the Hero Hall of Fame."

Abby had never thought of it in quite those terms,

but he was awful darn close to that in her book. Did that make him her significant other?

Nick gave Abby a sexy, teasing, beseeching look that made her warm all over. "Help me out here, pal. I have some credentials. Tell them how I saved Sarah's birthday party from disaster. Are you going to let her get away with this abuse?"

"Yes, you did. And yes, I am." The comment earned her laughter and nods of approval from the female members of his family.

Abby, towel in hand, stood with her back to the sink beside his mother, who was washing the oddball dishes that wouldn't go into the dishwasher. She took the cracked crystal bowl the older woman handed her.

"Ma," Nick said studying it, "are you ever going to tell us the story behind that bowl?"

"It's classified." His mother glanced over her shoulder and gave him an odd look. "A need-to-know basis. Right now you don't need to know."

He grinned. "Guess she told me."

"And don't you forget it," Rosie said. Her expression turned pensive. "Seriously, Nick, are you really all right?"

He sighed. "Abby, tell her."

She shrugged. "He joked about it with me. I have to conclude that the incident is behind him, emotionally speaking."

"I'm glad. But I still can't believe you kept it to yourself," Rosie said.

"That's not entirely true. I told Abby."

"You did?" Rosie and Flo said together as they stared first at him, then Abby.

"Yes. We're friends," he explained.

"Just good friends," Abby added. No doubt he'd

told Madison, too. Unfortunately she wasn't here to take the heat off.

"I know, but—" His mother didn't finish the statement, but there was no mistaking the gleam in her eye.

Because Nick seemed to have lost the power of speech, Abby scrambled to take the heat off all by herself. She searched for the first thing she could think of to say. "Did you know that Nick offered to let me use the cabin in the mountains while Sarah is nearby on a ski trip?"

"No," Flo said, giving her son an assessing look.

"Sorry, Ma," he said with a shrug. "I forgot."

"I hope that's all right with you?" Abby asked.

"Of course," Flo said.

"The cabin," Rosie said with a dreamy sigh. "That's where Steve and I fell in love. Remember, Nick?"

"I remember that I found the two of you in bed there before I found out you were married."

Rosie giggled. "I wish I had a picture of the look on your face."

"Very funny. I thought my best friend was taking advantage of my sister."

"And I wanted to strangle you for interrupting us on our honeymoon. We still had some things to work through then."

"And you did." Flo smiled at her daughter. "But that time at the cabin definitely brought you two closer. And now you're expecting another baby. True love seems to blossom there. Your father and I always thought of it as a romantic refuge."

Abby was uncomfortable with the direction of this conversation. "It was the treaty of Ridgeway for Sarah and me. Nick's idea. She's going on a church trip to the mountains. And I didn't want her to because I would worry like crazy. He thought I might be more comfortable if I was nearby.''

"Very thoughtful, Sir Galahad,'' his sister said.

"Apparently you didn't think it through completely,'' Flo commented. "If you don't clue your family in on this, your brothers could drop in on Abby.''

"Who's dumping on Abby?'' Joe asked. Lounging in the doorway between the kitchen and dining room, he seemed to fill the entrance.

"What's Abby doing?'' Alex said behind him.

"Who's picking on her?'' Luke questioned.

"I'm glad you're all here,'' Flo said. "Nick is letting Abby use the cabin for the weekend.''

"Great,'' Joe said. "Luke and I were thinking of going up. You busy, Alex?''

"No. I haven't been there in months.''

"We should do it. What do you say, Ab?'' Joe asked.

She grinned at the three of them. "Since it's your place, I don't feel I'm in a position to object.''

"You should,'' Nick said. His tone was light enough, but Abby noticed a tightness around his mouth and an intensity in his gaze that hinted at irritation.

She wondered what that was all about.

Joe walked farther into the kitchen and cut himself a piece of pumpkin pie, then sat at the table across from his brother. "What's eating you?'' he asked.

"Just that Abby never takes time off. She finally does, and has to share the place with a bunch of baboons like you guys? I don't think so.''

"It wouldn't bother me,'' she said.

"You think that now,'' he shot back. "But if—''

"It's really starting to rain,'' Flo said staring out the

window over the sink. "Abby, dear, do you have a four-wheel drive car?"

"No," she answered.

"Chains?" Joe asked.

She shook her head. "Why?"

Nick looked concerned. "Because if it's raining here, it could be snowing in the mountains."

Abby was a southern California girl, born and raised. She'd never set foot in the mountains or the snow and wasn't sure why all the Marchettis looked concerned. "Maybe I should have Sarah cancel her trip."

"Good luck," Nick said.

"But is it dangerous to drive?" she asked.

"Not if you're prepared," Alex answered.

"That settles it," Flo said.

Nick scratched his head. "I didn't realize there was anything to settle."

"Shows what you know," Rosie shot back. "I know where Ma's going with this."

"Then let me in on the secret," Abby said. "If necessary, Sarah and I will stay home."

"No, dear. That won't be necessary. Nick can borrow his father's Jeep, and he'll take you to the cabin tomorrow."

"He doesn't have to." Abby's heartbeat stuttered. "I'm sure I can handle the drive if I'm careful."

Rosie grinned. "Steve and Steph and I could come up, too. That way you wouldn't be alone with all of them, Abby."

Nick nodded, obviously warming to the notion. "We haven't hung out together in a long time. What a great idea, Ma."

It was a lousy idea, Abby thought. She couldn't handle much more of hanging around Nick Marchetti. Not if she wanted to hang onto her hard-won neutrality. "No, really," she protested. "I'd feel guilty about you driving me."

"Don't, Abby." Flo handed her a copper-bottomed pot to dry. "He's a notorious workaholic. He could use some time off, and you would give him a good reason. It would be a big favor to his family, friends, Marchetti's Inc., and the world in general. Please let him drive you to the mountains."

"Jeez, Ma, have I been that bad?" he asked, grinning at her.

"In a word? Yes," she said.

Abby didn't know what to say. But she didn't suppose that "no, you can't come," was an option. It was his cabin, after all. Not to mention the fact that he was going to make sure she arrived safely.

But she couldn't forget what his sister had said. The cabin was where she'd fallen in love. A romantic refuge, his mother had added.

"So what do you say, Ab?" Nick asked.

What else could she say with most of the Marchettis looking on? "Thank you very much."

Chapter Eight

"It's not the biggest, most impressive cabin I've ever seen." Abby tapped her chin as she studied the structure and the long wooden stairway leading up to it, rich in the ambience of the mountains.

"No?" Nick stood beside her, so close that their shoulders brushed.

The touch warmed her clear down to her toes. An impressive feat, she thought with a grin at her pun. A cleverness she would keep to herself because she didn't want to offer him the slightest bit of encouragement. After yesterday, she wasn't sure about anything. Even though she'd cautioned him not to have feelings for her, she sensed a restless tension in him. She hoped it wasn't about her, because she would never forgive herself if she was Nick's third strike in the romance department.

"Nope, definitely not the most impressive cabin I've ever seen. And if you believe that, I can probably convince you pigs can fly." She smiled up at him. "I've never been up close and personal with a mountain mansion. It's huge, Nick.''

"Wait till you see the inside," he said, walking to the rear of the sport-utility vehicle. His breath floated in a cloud in front of his face, attesting to the cold. He looked up at the gray sky. "Which I suggest we do real soon, before it starts in again. We were lucky it didn't snow harder on the way up the mountain."

"Okay." Good. Her voice had stayed steady. It was only one word, mind you. But one had to savor victories wherever one could. She was pleased that she hadn't betrayed any hint of her inner turmoil. Which she definitely had. Turmoil in spades.

Because she was alone with Nick.

Really and truly alone. Thanks to his mother, she thought, and didn't know whether to kiss or curse the woman. If Abby hadn't been put on the spot, she knew she would have taken her chances with the slick roads. But no such luck. So here they were. In the mountains, away from work. No phones, faxes or other related business paraphernalia to distract him, her, them. This was the moment she'd been anticipating with equal parts of trepidation and exhilaration.

When Nick finished taking the bags from the rear hatch of the car, Abby reached for her duffel.

Nick started to lift it at the same time. Their hands brushed, and she felt the sparks dance all the way up her arm until finally the warmth settled in her chest.

"I'll get that," he said.

Her knight in shining armor.

She thought of Nick's sister, teasing him. Then relief mixed with disappointment as she reminded herself that they would only be alone until his family arrived. Still, it was for the best that they wouldn't be by themselves for too long. Three whole days, one-on-one with Nick the magnificent, could be more than she'd bargained for. She was immensely relieved that her willpower wouldn't be put to the test so she decided to relax and make the best of a fabulous situation.

"You don't have to carry that. I'm perfectly capable," she said.

"I didn't mean to imply that you aren't." He held his hand out, indicating the stairway. "But it's a long way up, and the air here is thinner than you're used to. But have at it."

"I just want to pull my own weight," she said. "You did all the driving, and considering how slippery the roads were, that wasn't easy."

"No big deal." He shrugged. "Where I come from, guys take care of girls."

How wonderful, she thought. A man who was nice to his mother and a real gentleman. The woman who captured Nick Marchetti's heart would be lucky indeed.

Abby lifted her bag. "This isn't heavy," she said.

"I noticed. The women I know pack a truckload for a day. Are you sure you brought enough stuff?" He glanced down at her canvas sneakers. "Those are not going to keep your feet warm."

She shrugged. "I have a pair of athletic shoes, too."

"Better, but—" He shook his head as a frigid blast of wind hit them. "C'mon, let's get inside, out of this cold."

She shivered in her jacket. "You'll get no argument from me."

By the time they'd climbed the stairs, Abby was out of breath. Her chest felt tight, and she knew Nick hadn't exaggerated the effect of the altitude. He unlocked the door and let her go first.

She stepped into the living room and stared at the circular, screened-in fire pit that took up the center of the large room. On the walls around it sat a green plaid couch, matching love seat and occasional chairs in contrasting but compatible colors. There were oak tables nearby with lamps on top. It could have been put together by a decorator. Not to mention the fact that everything she saw was far superior to the furnishings in her apartment, and this was their home away from home.

"Wow. There must be a lot of loot in linguine."

He laughed. "I guess that means you like it."

"What's not to like?"

"It's pretty gloomy in here." It wasn't noon yet, but the clouds outside hid the sun, making the interior dark.

"Gloom is a relative term," she said.

"Relative to the fact that it's dark in here. But, never fear, Marchetti is here." Nick set his bag down, flipped the switch beside him, and instantly the lamps blazed with light.

"Wow," she said again. "It was pretty nice in the dark. But this is spectacular. Do you want to give me the nickel tour?"

"Your wish is my command."

Abby followed Nick into the spacious downstairs master bedroom complete with Jacuzzi tub and gold fixtures, walk-in closet and French doors leading to the balcony. After she grabbed her duffel, he showed her the second floor with its four bedrooms and loft filled with grown-up toys. She grinned at the pool table and dartboard, figuring that those distractions would appeal to manly men like the Marchettis.

"Which bedroom do you want?" Nick asked.

Her grin faded as other distractions that would ap-

peal to the Marchetti men and the women who were
attracted to them came to mind. Indoor sports. Man-
woman interaction. Kisses.

"Are there assigned rooms? I don't want to take
anyone else's and play Goldilocks and the Three Bears.
Your brothers will want to settle in when they get
here."

"Yeah." He thought for a minute. "Mom and Dad
are staying home with Grandma. If Rosie and Steve
make it, they'll want the master so they have room for
Stephanie in with them." He pointed down the hall.
"The one on the end is Rosie's old room. Why don't
you take it?"

"Joe and Alex and Luke won't mind?"

He shook his head. "Too girly."

"Okay."

"I'll put my stuff in the one next to it."

Was it too late to change her mind about Rosie's
room without looking foolish? she wondered.

"When the Three Bears get here, they can fight over
who gets to double up in the other rooms."

"If you say so," she said.

Three days with a testosterone level hovering near
the danger mark. Not an unpleasant prospect. But Abby
couldn't help wondering what it would be like to be
alone with Nick. Her heart gave a little skip at the
thought. As she'd said before, what's not to like? The
fact that she was a girl with a conscience. If she
weren't, she could enjoy him, then turn her back without a second thought. But he'd already been hurt by a
woman without a conscience. Abby couldn't do that to
him, not again.

"Why don't you unpack your stuff and settle in?"
he suggested.

"Nick, can we make sure the kids arrived safely first?"

"Not a problem. Just let me plug the phone into the jack downstairs. You can call—"

"I hate to ask this," she said. "But would you mind if we drove over to check out the lodge where they'll be staying? I know I'm a worrywart, pain in the neck, overprotective, et cetera. But the roads were so icy." She hesitated, waiting for him to laugh and tell her she was silly. When he didn't, she said, "I'd like to see for myself that Sarah's walking, talking, giggling and generally being her healthy sweet self."

"You got it." He didn't bat an eye or in any way indicate that her request was stupid.

Nick the Magnificent. He was hovering darn close to white-knight status. The next step was knight in shining armor, before he entered the Hero Hall of Fame. Abby feared that long before he reached those hallowed halls, he would hold her heart in his hand, and then she would be in a heck of a pickle.

Nick sat beside Abby in the café booth at the lodge as they waited for the church bus with the kids aboard.

"What if something happened?" she asked for the umpteenth time in a half hour as her worried gaze met his own.

"Don't borrow trouble, Ab."

"But it's snowing harder than ever. The roads are slippery. They left before us. They should have been here by now."

"Like I told you, buses go a lot slower than we did. Didn't you tell me the kids were stopping halfway for breakfast?"

She nodded, worrying her top lip with her teeth. "That's what the itinerary said."

"They could be two hours behind us," he said.

"Oh, Nick. I don't think I can stand much more." She folded her hands around the coffee cup in front of her. "I should never have let her go on this trip."

Nick stared at her, reminding himself that he didn't know what parenting felt like. He loved his niece, but he wasn't her primary caretaker, responsible for her upbringing and welfare twenty-four hours a day. He had no frame of reference for what degree of anxiety was acceptable in this situation. But he'd always believed it did no good to borrow trouble. And his gut told him that Abby was a degree or two above commonsense limits here.

Frowning, he studied her. The blond hair tucked behind her ears, the intensity in her eyes that turned them a darker shade of blue. Her lips, so full and tempting yesterday when he'd contemplated kissing her, now pulled tight with worry. He was afraid that if she didn't loosen the reins on her sister, there would be hell to pay.

"You did the right thing letting her go," he said. "You asked all the right questions, dotted all the *i*s and crossed the *t*s. I'm sure everything is going according to plan."

"No one planned for the snow. The icy roads were not on the itinerary. What if—"

"'What if' will give you an ulcer, pal."

Nick realized he wanted to make it better. He wanted to fix this problem and bring back the Abby he'd seen at the cabin a little while ago. That Ab had seemed relaxed and more carefree than he'd ever seen her. That woman had tested the limits of his willpower as he struggled not to take her in his arms and kiss her the way he wanted to.

But that would be borrowing trouble. Which he'd just decided was a bad idea. Especially when he could wind up with egg on his face again. He would have to be an idiot to pursue a woman who had come right out and told him that she wasn't interested in anything more than friendship. But he had to admit, the more she worried, the harder it was to keep from taking her in his arms. The more time he spent with her, the more certain he was that he cared for Abby. More than friendship, and more than he wanted to admit.

Nervously she brushed the hair off her forehead. Nick caught her hand between his own and rubbed her icy fingers. "Why don't I show you around town? We can call the lodge to see if the bus got here."

She shook her head. "I can't leave until I know she's all right."

"Then how about if I buy you some lunch? The last time I was here, I got a pretty good burger."

"You go ahead, Nick. I don't think I could eat a thing."

Abby had picked this booth for its clear view of the driveway, so that she could see when the bus arrived. He heard a rumbling like a truck at the same moment Abby pointed. As the big yellow vehicle lumbered past the window he read St. Ignatius Church on the side.

"There it is," she said. Her voice quivered with relief and excitement.

"Great. There's a little shop in the village I want to show you."

"No. I want to say hi to Sarah." She started to slide out of the plastic booth. "Then I'd love to see the village."

Nick put his hand on her arm. "Correct me if I'm wrong, but aren't you supposed to maintain a low profile? Sit on the bench in a supportive capacity in case you're needed? Hang out on the sidelines, not seen or heard unless called upon?"

"I'll do all of that. Just as soon as I touch base with my sister."

Once again, being the above-average-intelligent man that he was, Nick sidestepped the full-speed-ahead Abby Ridgeway. And he saw Sarah sitting inside the bus waiting her turn to get off. He watched her shoulders slump and a scowl replace her bright smile at the sight of her sister. He wished he'd stopped Abby. She was on a collision course with trouble. And he wanted to head her off at the pass.

The smell of exhaust was strong in the air as they stood by the bus watching the kids descend the stairs. Abby twisted her hands together as one by one the teenagers passed her. When Austin Reed climbed down and spotted them, he grinned.

"Hey, Nick." The tall teen looked at Abby. "Hi."

"Austin. How was the trip?" Abby asked.

"Great."

"No problems?"

"James got carsick. That was gross, but everything else was fine."

Sarah appeared in the doorway and Abby waved. "Hi, sweetie."

Nick wondered why the snow around little sister didn't melt, as hot as she looked.

"What are you doing here?" Sarah asked.

Instead of answering, Abby said, "How are you? Was the trip wonderful?"

"Can't you see I'm fine? No one else's parents

came. Would you please go away? Why do you have to embarrass me? Why can't I have some fun?'' she asked, her voice low, but tight with hostility. Sarah looked at him and pleaded, ''Nick, please take her somewhere and get her a life.''

He glared down at her. There weren't many years between the sisters, but since when had age lost its privileges? Abby had sacrificed her youth for this ungrateful little witch. ''That's no way to speak to your sister, Sarah.''

''It's all right, Nick—'' Abby touched his arm. ''Let her go.''

As he looked down at Abby, fighting the urge to say more, Sarah brushed past them and joined her friends on the way up the lodge steps. He decided it was best to let her go. Now wasn't the time to say what she needed to hear. But he wanted to shake some sense into the thoughtless teenager as he watched tears well in Abby's eyes, helpless to stop them. The term ''mixed feelings'' had never been more true. He was torn between annoyance at the inconsiderate teen and a clear understanding of why she'd needed to be independent. Then one fact stood out over everything and knocked the air out of him as surely as a punch to the gut.

He couldn't ignore his powerful need to protect Abby. He cared about her. A lot.

Not in a boss-employee way, and definitely more than as a friend. This wasn't the instantaneous, head-over-heels, blindsided sort of feeling he'd had for Margaret. Or the brotherly affection he had for Madison. This was different, and he wasn't sure he understood how or why. He only knew that he never again wanted to see her lips quiver as she struggled to keep from crying. No one, not even her sister, would hurt Abby if he could help it.

He put his arm around her, surprised but relieved when she let him lead her toward the Jeep. "C'mon. Let's go have some fun. I have a Twister game, and I know how to use it."

"My h-hero," she said, as her laugh caught on a sob.

With the key from the hook in the cabin kitchen, Nick unlocked the storage shed. He yanked on the string in the center and a light went on, illuminating the jam-packed space.

"I wonder where Dad put it," he said to Abby who followed him inside.

"What are you looking for?"

He pulled the saucer from a nail on the wall. "This."

She frowned. "It's a little big for a Frisbee, isn't it?"

Shaking his head, he sighed. "What am I going to do with you? It's time for footloose and fancy-free, the crash course."

"I'm not sure that's the best phrasing. Especially since I have a sneaking suspicion that you're going to make me do something with that contraption in the snow."

"Not to fear. I'll be with you every step of the way."

"Okay. Then let's take this baby out and see what she can do."

Nick switched off the light and locked up. Then, on impulse, he grabbed Abby's hand. "You don't have gloves."

She shook her head. "I didn't think about it. I had

no idea it would be so cold. I've never been in snow before."

He was torn between his concern for her and his need to make her laugh and take her mind off Sarah's hurtful words. Forgetfulness won. "Let's take a couple of runs down the mountain. Then we'll go into the village for dinner."

"Whatever you say."

He led her behind the cabin and positioned the saucer at the top of the hill. It was starting to snow again. Flakes caught in her hair and eyelashes. Clouds of white hovered in front of her as she blew on her hands. She'd never looked more appealing.

Before he did something he would regret, he sat down, spreading his legs to make room for her on the saucer. It *was* small, but still accommodated them both. Besides, it gave him the opportunity to be close to her. "Your chariot awaits, my lady," he said, holding out his arms to her.

Laughing, Abby settled in front of him. "Please tell me I'll live to regret this," she said, glancing over her shoulder at him.

"Have I ever lied to you?"

A sweet smile teased the corners of her full lips. "No. Never."

He tucked her hands beneath her armpits, then wrapped her in his arms. Holding her tightly to him, Nick whispered in her ear, "Then trust me. I won't let anything hurt you. And I promise you're going to love this."

Rocking his body forward started the saucer sliding down the hill. As they picked up speed, Abby squealed and hid her face against his forearms. Laughing, Nick shouted, "No guts, no glory."

They careened to the bottom, glanced off a snow-covered rock, and bounced into a snowdrift, laughing and unhurt. Eyes shining, cheeks red, Abby stood up. "That was great. Let's do it again."

"Last one to the top is a rotten egg," he said.

With the saucer in one hand and Abby's cold fingers in the other, he pulled her back up the hill. He laughed and Abby screamed as they went down again. After three more trips, he noticed that she was wet and shaking with cold.

"We better go inside and warm up."

"Just one more time, Nick. Please. I'm not cold." She blew on her reddened fingers. "R-really. Hardly at all."

"Yeah, I can tell." But he didn't have the heart to refuse her. So down they went one more time.

When they stood up, he noticed her hair had snow in it and hung in strands around her face. He also saw that her shivering was worse. But she had never looked more beautiful to him.

"No argument this time," he said. "We're going inside."

"Good idea. M-maybe your brothers are here."

Not if God was a man, Nick thought, trying to ignore the growing ache in his gut.

Chapter Nine

God was a man, Abby thought. No doubt about it. A female deity would have made sure that in her vulnerable-to-Nick state, she wouldn't be alone with him. But as yet there was no sign of his family.

Right now she relaxed in the upstairs tub, warming up after having the most fun she could remember in a very long time. And trying to figure out how to keep from falling in love with Nick. He'd been so sweet to her after Sarah's outburst. It was obvious that he wanted to play in the snow to take her mind off Sarah's nasty words. It had worked like a charm; darn tough to hold on to hurt feelings and your life at the same time.

He didn't even have to be in the same room to affect her heart rate. He was directly below, and she could hear the faint timbre of his voice as he sang in the shower. And she still had no one to run interference for her with Mr. Wonderful. And she meant that with all her heart. He *was* wonderful. Much too wonderful for her peace of mind.

The scene earlier with Sarah was an ugly black cloud hanging over her day. But there was a single silver lining. Nick had come to her rescue. She had carried the burden of raising Sarah for so long, that his support stood out like a lighthouse beacon on a particularly nasty, dark night at sea.

"My defenses are down. My hormones are clamoring to be set free. And we're alone. Where are the magnificent Marchettis when you really need them?" she asked helplessly.

She couldn't stay in the tub indefinitely. Not only was her skin turning all wrinkly, she was beginning to shiver again. The whole point of the bath was to warm up. At least that was Nick's point. Hers was to escape.

There was a single floor between them—he was showering in the downstairs bath. But that wasn't nearly far enough.

She heard the water shut off, and strains of a song drifted even louder through the floorboards. She tried to rein in her imagination, but the image of Nick, wet and slick with soap, and decidedly naked, took up residence in her mind. She tried valiantly to replace it with an ocean scene, but he managed to sneak his way in there, too—wearing a bathing suit. But it was skimpy and he was playing volleyball and those muscles she'd felt through his clothes rippled, naked and slick in the sun.

Stop it!

She sighed. "Maybe his brothers will be here soon," she said. "I just can't be alone with him."

There was a knock on the door. "Are you talking to yourself, Ab?"

Her heart hammered in her chest. He was on the other side of that door, semi-damp and probably semi-dressed. On her side of the door she was decidedly naked. She swallowed hard.

He knocked again. "Hey, are you okay? You didn't drown, did you? I thought I heard you talking to yourself."

"You did. My dark secret is out. But if you heard me sing, you'd be grateful that I'm just a little dotty."

"Hurry up. Your tour guide is getting restless. There's a whole village waiting for your perusal, my lady."

"Give me fifteen minutes."

"I'm going to start my watch. The timer starts—now."

"Okay. You're on."

Abby stood and grabbed a large thick towel that hung from a wall rack in front of her. She wrapped herself in the luxurious terry cloth and stepped out of the tub. Had Nick just rescued her again? A glow started in the pit of her stomach and radiated outward. It was as if he could read her mind and knew how nervous she was about being alone with him. He'd given her an out. They were going to the village.

The thought tugged at her heart and pricked her guilt. To a workaholic like Nick three days off were precious. He should be here with someone who could make him happy. Not stick-in-the-mud Abby. She wasn't free to pursue romance now. When her promise to raise Sarah was fulfilled, she would "get a life" as her sister had so bluntly put it. But for now the un-grateful little smart aleck would have Abby Ridgeway to deal with.

As she blew her hair dry, visions of herself with

Nick floated through her mind. It would be lovely if he waited until her responsibilities were behind her and they could pursue the feelings that simmered between them. But it wasn't fair to put his life on hold for her. He'd been badly hurt; he wanted a family. She'd seen the yearning on his face when his sister made her announcement about the new baby. He deserved to have all his dreams come true. A.S.A.P., not A.S.A.A.C.— as soon as Abby could.

Abby brushed a little blush onto her cheeks and some color on her eyelids. She slipped into her bedroom and put on the jeans and sweater she'd set out. After pulling on warm, dry socks and her sneakers, she took a last glance in the mirror. She looked pretty good. Anyone observing her and Nick together probably wouldn't conclude that he was slumming. Only she would know that emotionally that's exactly what was going on.

"You get three days' reprieve, Marchetti." She nodded resolutely at her reflection. "But time's awastin'. You're not getting any younger. When we get back to the real world, I'm going to rescue you. I'm going to find someone who can make you happy. Maybe Madison."

That thought made her deeply and profoundly sad.

Before she could dwell on it, there was a knock on her door. "My watch says one minute and ten seconds left. If you're going to make the deadline, you've got to stop talking to your invisible friend."

Abby laughed. Leave it to Nick to chase away the blues. "I'm ready," she said, opening the door.

He stood in the hall and the sight of him took her breath away. In his navy-and-gray plaid flannel shirt and worn jeans, he could have been the poster boy for lumberjacks. Her heart did a back flip. All the promises she'd made to herself flashed through her mind: always maintain a professional demeanor, never see Nick in anything but a suit and tie, above all never under any circumstances see him outside of work. And most especially, do not be alone with him.

She'd broken every single one of them. All at the same time. It was him, her, here and now in the cabin. But there was one promise to herself she wouldn't break. And she'd just made it. Find someone who's free, not to mention ready, willing and able to make his dreams come true as soon as possible.

She looked up at him and suppressed a sigh. "I'm ready."

He looked at his watch. "And with forty-five seconds to spare." He met her gaze and his eyes took on a hungry intense expression that was becoming familiar. "You look great, Ab."

The words nurtured her ego like water on a withering plant. "Thank you kind sir. But I bet you say that to all the girls."

"Only the ones I'm trying to impress." Before she could retort, he took her hand and said, "Let's boogie, beautiful."

Things were not going according to plan, Nick thought. He'd taken the girl out on the town, but all he could think about was getting her back to the cabin. And the activities he'd chosen hadn't helped take his mind off what he would like to do with Abby.

The late afternoon movie had been a romantic comedy. Judging by the glow in Abby's eyes as they'd left the theater, she had enjoyed it. He was glad about that, but it had enhanced ideas he was trying to forget. Now they were seated at the best restaurant the small alpine village had to offer. He wanted to buy her a nice dinner. Unfortunately, the best place to do that was also the most romantic in town.

Still, if it would take the edge off the way her day had started, with Sarah's spiteful words, and end it on a happy note, it would be worth a world of discomfort on his part. And he would be a lot worse off if they'd spent the evening alone at the cabin.

He was pretty sure she felt the same way. He'd seen the anxiety in her eyes after they'd finished playing in the snow, just before going back inside. She was afraid to be alone with him. But probably for different reasons.

He'd bet galoshes to snowshoes that she was completely innocent. He wanted her, more than he'd wanted any woman, and the ache was getting worse all the time. But she had never been with a man and that above everything would keep him in check. He had no intention of taking advantage of her. Getting her out into public places seemed the best way to put her at ease. He was starting to worry some about their chaperone squad.

He couldn't figure out what was keeping Joe, Alex and Luke. The weather had cleared. The roads were safe. The phone and message machine at the cabin were plugged in and operational. They hadn't received any word on his brothers' estimated time of arrival. He figured they'd probably just gotten a late start. No doubt when he and Abby returned to the cabin, the place would be crawling with Marchettis.

In the meantime, he could wine and dine her and make her feel special. His need for her would no doubt pick up speed like an avalanche, but his brothers presence would dig him out. It was sort of like walking a tightrope with a net.

When the waiter brought his beer and her wine, he ordered dinner for both of them without asking for menus.

A frown marred the smooth skin of her forehead, but she didn't say anything until after the waiter walked away.

"Nick, it makes me nervous when I don't see a menu."

"Don't worry about it."

"Easier said than done. I'd like to know how many dishes I'll have to wash before they let me leave."

He frowned. "No one's washing dishes, and you're not leaving—at least not until you've had dinner."

"What are you saying, Nick?"

"That you were right. There is a lot of loot in linguine." He took a sip of his beer. "And I intend to spend some of it on you tonight."

"I can't let you pay for everything. It wouldn't be right."

"Why not? It's what a guy usually does for his date."

Her hand froze as she reached for her wine. "Date?"

"Yeah. A guy. A girl. A movie. Dinner. It has all the essential elements."

"Not all. You need a guy and a girl who are looking to get serious."

"Not necessarily. It's when a guy and a girl try each other out to see if they *want* to get serious. Your education in this area is sadly lacking, Ab."

"I don't dispute that. But my vocabulary is pretty good. And I can't call this a date. I don't do that."

"So you've said. But just so you recognize it in the future, this is what it feels like."

She shook her head. "You can dangle the carrot, but it's not in my foreseeable future."

"You might want to re-think that."

"I don't have time—"

He took her hand in his. "The guys you knew had to be a bunch of jerks. Like I said—don't look now. But I just lined up all your ducks in a perfect row. If we weren't just friends, we could be on a date. If I can arrange it, so can anyone else."

"Oh, Nick. This is terrible."

"Why?" he asked totally at a loss.

"Date implies further...excursions."

Interesting choice of words. He couldn't wait to see where she was going with this.

"You are absolutely right. Date definitely implies further togetherness."

"I can't do that."

"I beg to differ. For the next two days you can kick up your heels, and I'd be happy to help you do graduate work in footloose and fancy-free."

"What about Sarah?"

"She's not a traumatized eleven-year-old anymore, Ab. She doesn't need you in the same way. She's a young woman who's trying to spread her wings."

"And it's my job to channel her flight when she does."

"Agreed. But she needs space to fly. Your parents wouldn't want you to sacrifice your own life. They would want you to find someone and be happy."

"Like they were?" She snapped the words out.

Nick knew she hadn't meant to tell him that. There-

fore it got his attention in a big way. "There were
problems?" he asked gently.

She hesitated for so long, he thought she wasn't going to answer. Finally, she made a small movement
with her head, not quite a nod, but still affirmative.

She sighed. "They got married very young, eighteen. My mother was pregnant with me. The marriage
lasted because of me. But as I got older it began to
deteriorate. She was going to leave my father when she
discovered she was going to have another baby.
Sarah."

She stopped, and he wondered if she would say
more. He got the feeling that she hadn't told anyone
else about this. This was a heavy load for anyone, let
alone someone so young.

"Go on," he encouraged.

"There was a lot of fighting. I don't think Sarah
knew, or she doesn't remember. But they had decided
to split." A pained expression crossed her face and for
a brief moment she closed her eyes. "Before the final
decision, they reluctantly agreed to go away together,
to see if there was any way to salvage the marriage."
She sighed, a big sad sound. "They never came back."

"Abby," he said, then tightened his hold on her
hand. "I don't know what to say."

"You don't have to say anything." She shrugged,
looking so young, so vulnerable, so incredibly sad.

Not much different from the first time he'd seen her.
He remembered that day, when she'd promised to be
the best employee he'd ever had. Fresh from his own
rejection, he hadn't noticed what was going on with
her the way he should have. If he hadn't been so selfish, burying his feelings so no one could hurt him
again, he would have seen that she was doing the same

thing. But he'd been the only reveler at a pity party that had lasted way too long. And she had forfeited five years of her life.

Maybe if he hadn't been so self-absorbed he could have helped her. Maybe they could have helped each other.

He wished he could give her back the time she had lost.

Her revelation about her parents helped him understand a few things. Like the fact that she'd been hiding behind her obligation to Sarah. Maybe that was part of the reason she was trying so hard to prevent Sarah from growing up. It would keep her from having to put her heart on the line.

In the last five years Abby's situation had worked to scare guys off. But Nick didn't frighten easily. He was five years late, but he could still help her. He would show her that she could date if she wanted to. Time management was the key.

He would also tutor her in the dos and don'ts of dating. She was a babe in the woods where guys on the make were concerned. The thought of innocent Abby at the mercy of an octopus with eight hands made him crazy. Since he wouldn't always be around to protect her, he would arm her with knowledge. He hated the idea of her with another guy, but he was damaged goods. She deserved someone who could love her. And too much time had been wasted already.

He would see her safely on the road to fancy-free, or his name wasn't Nick Marchetti.

Chapter Ten

"So, do you want me to call you Don Juan or Casanova?" Abby asked.

"It's just role-playing. Sir, your honor, or your worship will do just fine."

She laughed. "No, really, Nick. I need to get into my role. What's my motivation—"

Nick's glare silenced her. "You're not taking this seriously at all, are you?"

"Neither are you."

Abby set the pan of chicken she'd just breaded into the oven. She met Nick's phony annoyed gaze and raised him a saucy stare. He was putting the finishing touches on a salad to go with their main course. It had been twenty-four hours since their lovely date— No! Not date. Never a date. She wouldn't even think that.

It had been a friendly dinner. One that had gotten a little too personal for her peace of mind. She hadn't meant to blurt out that her parents had been on the brink of a break-up when they'd died in the car accident. She usually managed to put that out of her mind. Because guilt followed when she recalled her role in that.

But for some reason, after last night, Nick had decided she needed tutoring in what the teenagers called "going out." He'd called it Dating 101, or the ups and downs, ins and outs and general survival techniques for a single woman in the nineties. The whole thing made her uncomfortable. Especially since they were still alone.

Nick had phoned his parents for information on his brothers' estimated time of arrival, but no one had answered. He didn't seem too worried. He'd said if there was a problem they would get word. So, they continued to be by themselves. Sleeping in rooms that were separated by one, thin wall. If you could call it sleeping. She'd tossed and turned, and when she wasn't doing that she was dreaming about Nick.

That was what had convinced her to go along with his tutoring idea. It could come in handy. For her. She wasn't worried about Nick. He seemed perfectly content to maintain the parameters they'd set up.

And that thought disturbed her more than a little.

But what was she supposed to think? He hadn't even kissed her. The pesky little voice inside tried to warn her that thinking along those lines was one step from disaster. But she tried to be more optimistic. Life *was* a series of pitfalls. If she kept her eyes wide open and on the road in front of her, she could avoid bottoming out. Since she was already here with Nick, and through no fault of hers they were still alone, she decided to make the best of the best situation she could imagine. Tomorrow she would worry about disengaging herself.

Tonight she could still fret about why he hadn't kissed her.

Right now her modus operandi was teasing him.

"I'm taking this as seriously as you are, Your Worship." She looked up at him. "Explain to me again what 'this' is."

"You need an intensive seminar on the dating scene. After last night's dinner conversation, it became clear to me that you need some instruction in this sort of thing. You're a target for every Lothario who comes down the pike."

"Aha. Your worship isn't good enough for you. Now you want me to call you Lothario. Does the phrase 'multiple-personality disorder' mean anything to you?"

"Seriously, Ab. The longer you go without dating, the more vulnerable you become."

"Why?" She couldn't help glowing over the fact that he looked really worried. About her.

"Guys will assume you know the ropes. They'll hit on you and figure you know the score and will handle the situation like a woman of experience. Only you've never done it before, so you're a babe in the woods. And every wolf on the make will be after you."

"Wolf?"

"All guys are half man, half wolf. They're on the prowl, predators who take no prisoners. They'll chew you up and spit you out." He grinned suddenly. "Unless you follow Nick Marchetti's three simple rules."

"What if I *want* their advances?"

His smile disappeared, replaced by a thundercloud of a frown. "That's another seminar, entitled Try That Again and You'll Be Singing Soprano."

She giggled, very much liking his protective attitude. "Okay. What do I say to a guy?"

"No."

She blinked. "We can't talk about what to talk about? That's my biggest weakness. What do I say to a guy?" she asked again.

"No. I meant you always tell a guy no."

"Always?"

"No matter what," he said, slam-dunking the cucumbers he'd just sliced into the lettuce. "Without question. Do not pass go, just tell him no. *N-o.* Period. End of conversation."

She opened the drawer and pulled out two place mats and arranged them across from each other at the pine table. Turning back she asked, "Then how am I ever going to get a date? If I say 'no' when someone asks me out, my footloose-and-fancy-free phase will last about thirty seconds."

"That wouldn't be so bad," he mumbled.

"What?"

"That would be so sad." He began to chop celery with a bit more enthusiasm than the job warranted. He was certainly peeved about something.

"Okay so how do I talk to a guy? What do you like to talk about?"

"Books, movies, that perfume you wear."

"You like it?" she asked.

"Oh, yeah."

She met his gaze and the look he sent her made her hot all over. Shaking, she did a quick about-face toward the cupboard to pull out some plates. "I'm glad. It was recommended by—"

"Never under any circumstances wear it on a date," he said sharply.

"Really?" His comment froze her and she turned back to look at him. "Why?"

"It gives a guy ideas," he said.

"Like what?"

He met her gaze and there was an expression in his eyes—a hunger that she would swear had nothing to do with food. "Just never you mind," he answered, his voice husky and just this side of a growl. "One hurdle at a time. Although if you follow my simple rules, you should sail through without a problem."

His look made her insides quiver and her heart pound like a stereo with too much bass. "Okay. What are the rules?" she asked breathlessly.

"Number one—no matter how great a guy seems, he always wants something."

"Of course he does. A good time."

"No kidding." He gave her a wry look.

"I know we're talking about two different things here. But seriously, isn't the whole point of dating to have a good time?"

"Yes. But there's a good time." He raised one dark eyebrow suggestively. "And there's a good time," he said, lowering his voice to a seductive growl that sent shivers of delight down her spine.

"Okay." She swallowed. Kissing would definitely be part of that second "good time" he was talking about. She wanted to know what the rest of it entailed. She desperately wanted Nick to tutor her in all of the above. With an effort, she brought herself back to the conversation. "I—I think I get your drift. What else?"

"Never under any circumstances go with a guy to his place."

She looked around the well-appointed kitchen and

just couldn't help asking, "You mean like we are now?"

"Yes," he said automatically. Then he looked startled. "I mean no. This is different."

"How?"

Abby found that she didn't want it to be different. She wanted to be a couple, like the ones she'd envied when she first started working at Marchetti's. She desperately wanted to *not* feel alone. All she could think about was being in his arms, with his mouth on hers.

"How is this different?" she asked softly.

"My mother told me to take care of you, Abby. Besides, this is you and me. We're just different," he said with a shrug. "What I meant was after a romantic dinner, if your date asks you back to his place to see his etchings, that's a definite no."

"Do you have any etchings, Nick?" she asked.

He looked momentarily startled, then shook his head. "Not unless you count the manufacturer's name engraved on my free weights."

He lifted weights? Moron, she said to herself. Of course he did. There was a reason he had that washboard stomach. She'd felt the strength in his arms as he'd held her when they went careening down the snow-covered hill.

"Can I see them?" she asked. A fluttering started in her abdomen.

"You want to see my free weights?"

She hesitated trying to decide whether to be honest or say no. Finally, she nodded. "And if you showed them to me," she wondered out loud, "what are the rules about kissing?" She stood several steps away from him with her back to the refrigerator.

"Kissing?" His eyes smoldered as he set his paring

knife down on the butcher-block cutting board and wiped his hands on the dishtowel. He stared at her for several moments and her heart pounded as anticipation pumped adrenaline through her. His long stride chewed up the small distance between them in less than a heartbeat.

"Never let a guy corner you," he said placing his hands on the refrigerator on either side of her head.

Their bodies barely touched. She wanted more. She wanted to lean into him, press her aching breasts against his hard chest. She was desperate to feel his arms come around her, then pull her closer as if he would never let her go.

"And if he does?"

"If it's me, you do this," he said, lowering his head.

Abby held her breath, every second exquisite torture, until he touched his mouth to hers. His lips were firm yet soft, sweet but with a hint of fire that stole the air from her lungs. When he traced her upper lip with his tongue, she opened her mouth and he slipped inside to caress the warm moisture. Her already pounding heart increased tempo.

She didn't think her reeling senses could take more, but found out she was deliciously wrong when he shifted his attention from her mouth to her neck. Correction: one hypersensitive spot just beneath her ear. The featherlight brush of his lips sent an arc of electricity zinging through her.

She slid her hands up, over his chest, and wrapped them around his neck, loving the way he felt—strong, solid, sexy. If there were truly rules to a situation like this, she wanted to break every last one of them with Nick. She trusted him completely. In fact, she tipped her head to the side giving him room to keep on doing what he was doing because she never wanted the sensations cascading through her to stop.

But he lifted his head and looked at her, his chest rising and falling rapidly. How she wished she already had the experience he was trying to teach her. What should she say? "Don't stop" worked for her.

She dropped her arms and laughed a little shakily. "And the rule you were showing me would be?" she asked, desperately trying to keep her voice light.

He stared down at her his eyes dark with intensity. "There are no rules for that. It wasn't a game. It was for real—and for keeps."

She knew exactly what he meant. She felt the same way. But she had no frame of reference that included "for keeps." Nothing was forever. It was foolish and just asking to get kicked in the teeth to even try.

She couldn't kiss him anymore. She couldn't let this continue. For his sake—and her own.

Taking two steps away, she turned and reached into the still-open cupboard for the plates. Her hands were shaking. "Thanks for the tips, Nick. When I'm ready to date, they'll come in handy."

"Abby, I—"

"Don't say anything. Please," she begged, squeezing her eyes shut as if she could close out his sensory barrage and the temptation along with it. "I don't want to talk about this."

Even with the space between them she felt his tension. Finally he said, "Okay. For now." There was an edge to his voice that she'd never heard before. "But you can't keep running. Sometime soon, we're going to have to talk about it."

She turned slowly and met his gaze. The look in his eyes scared her. She never wanted to put into words the power of what had passed between them. She wasn't even sure she could. They had crossed some kind of line tonight. Stepped off a cliff, free-falling and reaching for each other. If she had to put it into a coherent thought, she would be forced to admit that she was falling for Nick Marchetti.

She absolutely, positively could not love him. Correction: she would not under any circumstances, in any way shape or form, be *in* love with him.

They were so out of sync. He was looking for a till-death-do-us-part relationship. She hadn't yet experienced the hey-babe-what's-your-sign phase. She had already told him she intended to do footloose before settling down. But it was more than that. She wouldn't date until she had the time to participate in single-girl stuff so she would know the right guy when he came along.

Her parents were each other's first and they'd had to get married. She didn't want to repeat that mistake. They'd been on the verge of splitting up. If and when she got married, she wanted it to be right—to be forever. Her plan required a long stretch of free time. And that was months away. She couldn't afford to count on Nick being there for her. Nothing serious could happen between them, even though her heart was telling her to go full-speed ahead in that very direction. Nick knew how much she wanted to be part of a family. It was possible that his interest was nothing more than an overactive sense of duty. To continue what they'd just started would only hurt him in the long run. That was something she would never, ever do.

She would do whatever was necessary to avoid being his strike three.

* * *

Nick heard his cuckoo clock chime 1:30 a.m. Lounging in his favorite old chair in his condo, he brooded over what to do about Abby. In the several weeks since their mountain weekend, he'd discovered that getting her out of his mind wasn't an option. He hadn't seen or talked to her since he'd dropped her off that Sunday, but he'd thought about little else ever since. He'd hoped if he gave her time and space she would come to her senses and contact him.

"No such luck," he said, staring distastefully at the warm, long-neck beer bottle in his hand. He'd opened it hours before and hadn't even tasted it.

Something told him he was going to have to make the first move with Abby, if there was going to be one. Did he want to?

Oh, yeah. The answer came without hesitation. Was it logical? *No way* came the answer just as swiftly.

He'd known Abby for a long time, but only recently had he noticed sparks flying. When he fell for a woman it was fire at first sight. She was obviously wrong for him. But he couldn't get that message from his mind to his gut. It was telling him to remember that kiss.

If they hadn't spent the three days alone, it never would have happened. His brothers had given him vague excuses for not showing up. Not that it mattered now. The damage was done. They'd been alone, and he'd kissed her. That had shifted the emotional thermostat between them up to the high end of serious sizzle. After that, she had retreated behind walls she couldn't erect fast enough, starting with her commitment to Sarah and ending with his relationship with Madison. Which he kept reminding her was ancient history.

As hard as he tried, he couldn't forget what had happened at the cabin. She had kissed him like a woman whose heart was tied to his. He knew Abby. She didn't play games. If her kiss said she cared, then she cared. Whether or not she would admit it was something else again.

He wanted to find out if something special between them stood a chance. But could he get past his own painful past to take the step he knew she wouldn't?

Which brought him back to the question at hand. To see her, or not to see her. To call or not to call.

The phone rang suddenly, startling him. He thought about not picking up. But it was late and must be important. He grabbed the receiver. "Hello."

"Nick! Thank God."

"What's wrong?"

"Sarah's not home. I'm so afraid something's happened to her."

"Don't borrow trouble, Ab." That was the second time he'd told her that. He was beginning to see a pattern forming. She always went to the worst-case scenario. "If something bad had happened, you would know," he said. He sat up in the chair, all his senses on full alert, adrenaline pumping.

"I don't know what to do, Nick." Her voice broke on a sob.

"I'll be right over," he said.

"You don't have to—"

"Yeah, I do. I'll be there in fifteen minutes."

Abby answered the door even before he knocked. He knew by the way her expression turned from anticipation to disappointment that she'd hoped he was Sarah. That told him there was no news yet.

"I've called around, Nick. I've left messages with everyone I could think of."

He walked into her apartment and closed the door. "Tell me what's going on."

She tipped her head to the side and looked at him, puzzled. "I already told you. Sarah hasn't come home."

He shook his head. "I mean what happened to set this off."

"What makes you think something happened?"

"Because I know Sarah. She's basically a good kid."

"Are you implying that I did something? You think she's run away?"

"No, I don't think that. But did you two have an argument about something?"

"Of course not. I'm the adult. She's the child. I set the rules."

Sarah wasn't a child, but that was another discussion. "So there were words between you."

"I suppose you could call it that," she said.

"Wasn't tonight the winter formal?" he asked. Sarah had talked to him about it and the fact that it was a special occasion so she should be able to stay out later.

Abby caught her top lip between her teeth as she nodded. "She went with Austin."

"Did you argue about something?"

"We discussed her curfew."

"Tell me you extended it."

"This was a special occasion. Of course I did. She was supposed to be in the door at twelve-thirty." She glanced worriedly at the watch on her wrist. "She always comes in on time."

"Did you check with any of the other parents to see when they wanted their kids home?"

"I did. But Sarah's only sixteen. I thought two-thirty was a bit late."

He looked at his own watch. "It's nearly that now."

Abby started pacing. "I'm so worried about her. Why hasn't she called? If she's okay, she would have called."

"When you 'discussed' her curfew, did it turn into a fight?"

She sighed, a sound that was just this side of a sob, then nodded. "Yes. This morning. When I drove her to school. But before she left for the dance, everything seemed fine. Austin picked her up, and he said he would have her home on time."

"I have a theory," he said.

"What, Nick?"

"What if she told Austin that she could stay out until two-thirty? There's a very good chance she didn't want to be the only one attending who had to be home early."

"Sarah wouldn't lie. Besides she knows I would know and she would get in trouble."

"Maybe it's worth it to her."

Should he tell her that he'd already caught Sarah doing something he knew Abby wouldn't approve of? It might give her a little peace of mind, but Sarah would be in a lot more trouble. He decided to bide his time on that one.

"No." She shook her head. "If she's not home, it's because she can't be."

"It's possible they had a flat tire, or ran out of gas." Nick thought that was unlikely. And if that's what had kept them, they could have called.

"What if there's been a car accident?" Abby said.

"I can't help thinking of her out there alone, hurt, needing help. Needing me."

When her face drained of color, Nick went to her and pulled her into his arms. Violent tremors shook her from head to toe, and he thought she was going to collapse. He guided her to the love seat and sat down, tugging her onto his lap so he could hold her. He rubbed some warmth into her arms. It was as if she was cold from the inside out.

"If anything bad had happened, you would have heard."

"Not necessarily. The authorities have to determine who the victims are. Notifying next of kin can be difficult. If ID isn't readily available, they have to check license plates. It could be hours—"

"Don't go there, Ab. I'm sure it's nothing like that."

Nick held her tighter. She had been through the worst thing a kid could experience. Of course she would leap to the worst case scenario. How could he help her see that she was jumping to conclusions? Nine times out of ten there was a perfectly reasonable explanation for things.

"Nick, she's all I have in the world. I can't lose another person I care about." She said the last part so low he almost didn't hear the words. But the pain was there in every softly spoken syllable.

"I'm sure your sister is fine."

The trauma she had suffered was still with her. She lived it every day. It was compounded by the fact that she was responsible for the only family she still had left.

Abby, how can I help you? What can I do to convince you that lightning almost never strikes the same place twice?

This wasn't the time, but he wanted to say that Sarah wasn't the only person she had in the world. She had him. She would always have him. He knew now that he could have sat alone forever and brooded about whether or not to contact her. But the decision was never really in question. His feelings had gone from respect and admiration to hotter than an out-of-control forest fire. Not his usual way, but facts were facts. And the fact was, Abby had become an important part of his life. Being without her was like not having air to breathe or food to eat. And when she had phoned him, he'd gone without hesitation.

He was in love with Abby.

But right now, he had to help her get through what he felt sure was nothing more than teenage rebellion. Then he would tell her how he felt.

Just then, there were voices outside. The sound of a key in the lock. The door opened and Sarah walked in. "Good night, Austin. Thanks for everything. I had a wonderful time."

Nick took in Sarah's spaghetti-strapped, royal-blue dress and realized how grown-up she was. Her upswept hair, white-rose wrist corsage and dramatic night makeup all combined to add at least ten years. Not to mention the glow on her face—until she met her older sister's gaze. Then the shutters closed, replaced by a sullen, rebellious look.

Abby stood up. "I want to talk to him."

Sarah quickly shut the door and stood in front of it. "He's gone."

"Are you okay, sweetie? Did something happen?"

"Of course not." Sarah met Nick's gaze and smiled. "Hi. What are you doing here?"

"I called him because I was frantic. You scared me

to death. All kinds of things went through my mind when you didn't come home. I'm going to call Austin's mother and give her a piece of my mind.''

"Don't you dare,'' Sarah said, her eyes flashing. "It's my fault. I told him I could stay out later. If you want to ground me for the rest of my life, go ahead. I don't care. Just because you don't want to have a life doesn't mean I won't. At least for one night I got to have a good time like all the other kids. I don't want to be a lonely old maid like you. I hate you,'' she said, then ran from the room.

Nick decided a cooling-off period was a must before he told her that her behavior was inappropriate. Tomorrow he and a certain teenage girl were going to have a chat.

Abby couldn't have looked more shocked if Sarah had slapped her. She turned to him. "I'm glad she's okay, because tomorrow I'm going to kill her.'' She breathed in, a shuddering sound.

"Not if I get to her first.'' He despised the thought of Abby going through even a moment of anxiety, and he intended to see that it never happened again.

"She lied to me. You were right.''

"Try to see her side. She's growing up. You said yourself that she'll be off to college pretty soon. In spite of the fact that you want to keep her a little kid. She needs to have more freedom under controlled circumstances to prepare her to be on her own.''

"That's a tough one for me, especially after she just proved to me how she handles more freedom. Lying?'' She shook her head in disbelief.

"It's not the first time,'' he said gently. She needed to know that her tight parameters were driving Sarah in the wrong direction.

Her eyes grew wide. "How do you know?" she asked sharply.

"She talks to me."

"What else has she done?" Her voice was deadly calm and cool.

"She took a ride from a recently licensed driver. Nothing serious."

"You don't think that's serious?" Her face turned pale, like it did when she'd remembered how her parents died. "Now she lied to me and stayed out late."

"Only as late as the other kids. Probably not a hanging offense," he said, hoping to coax a smile out of her. No such luck. "I'm sorry I didn't tell you sooner. I guess I should have. But I understand where she's coming from."

"You think I can't?"

"No, because when you should have rebelled, you became mother and father to her. You never had the freedom of opportunity." He ran a hand through his hair. "I've tried to talk to you about this. Abby, you have to make an effort to put yourself in her shoes. You can't keep her on such a tight leash."

"I'm trying to protect her." She looked up at him.

"I know you are, honey. But smothering her isn't the way." He reached for her, intending to pull her into his arms.

Fear flashed through her eyes just before she took a step back. "Nick, it's late and I'm tired. Not to mention angrier than I've probably ever been in my life at the two most important—" She stopped and dragged in a deep breath. "I think you should go."

He frowned. "We should talk about this."

"There's nothing further to say. By keeping that confidence, you encouraged Sarah's deception. It's a behavior that could have been a disaster. How would you have felt if she had been in an accident tonight?"

"Awful. I don't know. I—"

"You're right. I don't know how to rebel. But I do know what it feels like to lose your whole world. And I'll do whatever I can to keep it from happening again."

"Abby, let me help."

"You've already done enough." She went to the door and opened it. "I appreciate you coming over so late. Thank you, Nick. Now it's time to say goodnight."

He shook his head, puzzled and disturbed. "That tone in your voice. It smacks of 'don't darken my doorway again.'"

"Maybe that's not such a bad idea."

Nick was stunned. He was afraid to breathe. Afraid if he did the pain would come and bring him to his knees again. "You don't mean that, Abby."

"Yes," she said, meeting his gaze directly. "I do mean it. Goodbye, Nick."

Chapter Eleven

Abby curled up in the corner of the couch and prayed that the cup of coffee wrapped in her hands would take the place of the whole night's sleep she'd lost. She couldn't shake the bad feeling that had settled over her.

From the corner of her eye, she saw movement in the hall. Her sister was finally up. She was dreading another confrontation.

Sarah sat down on the love seat, looking sulky, sullen, and as sleepy as Abby felt. "I'm sorry about last night, Abby."

"Me, too. And you're still grounded."

"Why would you lighten up on me just because Nick says you should?"

"This is between you and me, Sarah. Why can't you understand that I'm just trying to do the best job I can to finish what Mom and Dad started?" She felt tears burn the back of her eyes. "And I stink at it."

Sarah's face clouded. "And why can't you understand that I feel guilty every time you don't go out because of me? If I was eighteen right now, I'd move out. Then you wouldn't have to worry about me.''

"I love you, Sarah." Abby's stomach knotted at the thought of losing the only family she had left. "I'll always worry about you. You're all I've got."

"You've got Nick."

Abby shook her head. "He's just my boss."

"He's stuck on you, Abby. But I overheard what you said to him. You need to talk to him."

"There's nothing more to say."

Sarah stood up, the rebellious look back. "Yeah, there is. You care about him, too. He can show you how to have a good time."

"So I'll lighten up on you?" Abby said, trying to coax a smile from her sister.

"No. Maybe. But mostly it's about you. Don't make me your whole life. What are you going to do when I'm all grown up, Abby?" She turned and ran from the room.

Abby finally realized what that bad feeling was. She felt like she was losing her whole world. Again.

As soon as the door had closed behind Nick, she'd had a flash of comprehension. She was in love with Nick Marchetti. But that was impossible. Or was it? She hadn't spent any significant time with him. Or had she? Wasn't it possible that falling in love happened in a less than orderly way like her parents? They'd had more good times than bad in spite of the way they got together. If they'd lived, they might have salvaged the marriage. She couldn't make him happy.

That thought broke her heart.

Standing at the restaurant podium, Abby looked up from checking her dinnertime waiting list. Madison

Wainright walked up to her. "Abby, could I speak with you?"

"Of course," Abby answered automatically. Shock at seeing the other woman had momentarily cut off the blood supply to her brain.

She had a feeling she didn't really want to have this conversation. She was fairly certain she wouldn't like what Madison was here to say. If she and Nick had patched things up, that would be good news and bad. Bad because Abby had realized that she loved him. Good because if he was happy with Madison, she, Abby, couldn't hurt him any more than she already had.

After her anger had abated, she was appalled at how she'd sent him away. Countless times she had picked up the phone to apologize. Then what? She would be right back where she'd started. Loving him with nowhere to go. She'd decided that since the deed was done, it was best to leave it that way. If only she didn't see the future in black and white. Without Nick, all the color had disappeared from her world. She was left with profound emptiness and an ache that didn't go away, not even in sleep.

"Why don't we go somewhere quiet?" she said, indicating the hall leading to the manager's office.

"I'm not taking you away from work, am I?" Madison asked, looking around the sparsely filled restaurant.

Abby looked at her watch, then shook her head. "It's past the dinner rush. And rush is definitely the right word. My feet are killing me. This way," she said.

Abby led the way to the quiet room in the rear of Marchetti's. "Have a seat," she said, sitting behind the desk.

Madison gracefully took one of the chairs facing her. "I'd like to talk to you about Nick."

Abby's heart contracted at the sound of his name on the other woman's lips. "Yeah. I didn't figure you were here to discuss the price of pasta."

Madison smiled. "No. That's not my area of expertise."

"Before you start, I just want to reassure you that Nick and I are nothing more than friends." Liar! Not only did she love him, but they didn't even have friendship anymore. "You have nothing to worry about on my account."

"Funny, that's what I was going to tell you."

Abby blinked as she let the words sink in. "Excuse me? What did you say?"

"Nick and I are just friends. You have nothing to worry about from me."

"But you guys are just taking a break from each other. You'll get back together. If you give it a chance, I'm sure you can work out whatever the problem is."

"I don't think so."

"Madison, you can't give up on this. You won't find a better man than Nick. He's loyal, funny, smart, good-looking enough to tempt a saint." Abby figured the years of all work and no play had finally made her crazy. Why else would she sell another woman on the man she loved? Because she wanted him to have the wife and family he'd longed for.

"Yes, he's everything you say and more."

"Then what's wrong? I didn't peg you for a quitter. You don't get through law school by giving up on your briefs. You have to try. If you don't, you'll break his heart again."

"Again?" Madison looked confused.

"Yeah, you know. Like that moron in Phoenix that he married."

Her confusion cranked up a notch. She looked ready to call the guys in the white coats. "What are you talking about, Abby?"

"You remember. He told you. The woman who was pregnant with another man's baby. The one he married to give her and the baby a name. Then the bozo came back and she dumped Nick—"

Her gasp of stunned surprise was no act. She really and truly had no idea what had happened. Nick hadn't confided in her. Oh lord, that meant she, Abby, *was* the first person he had told. That meant—that meant stuff she didn't want to think about.

"No, Abby. I didn't know. Poor Nick. He's always trying to take care of everyone. He needs someone to protect him from himself."

"He has you," Abby said, really getting nervous now.

Madison shook her head. "No. I did the right thing when I broke it off."

"But he cares about you."

The other woman shrugged. "As a friend. That's not good enough for me. Besides, there would always be another woman standing between us."

"Who?" Abby had to ask even though she knew what the other woman would say.

"It's you, Abby."

She shook her head. "No. It can't be me. I'm completely wrong for him."

Madison lifted one shoulder in a half shrug. "Says who? If he isn't in love with you, he's awfully close."

"I don't want him to care about me. I've been trying so hard to prevent this very thing." Abby stood. "Madison, you've got to go after him. He's been hurt twice and once was you.''

"The last thing I want is a Marchetti man.'' She shook her head vehemently. "Besides, I didn't hurt him. But you'll break his heart if you don't stop burying your head in the sand and take what he's offering.''

"I can't have him.'' Abby felt a rising wave of panic, mixed with a healthy dose of pain. Why couldn't things have been different?

"I don't understand what's standing in your way, Abby. It's obvious to me that you care about him very much.'' She stood up, too.

"Did Nick put you up to coming here?'' Abby asked.

"No. But I saw him recently. I'm on retainer for Marchetti's Inc. He looked like he hadn't slept in weeks. Your name happened to come up in conversation.''

"My name?''

She nodded. "I don't remember why. But he said that you're under the mistaken impression that he and I are still an item. I'm here to tell you that's not true.''

"You could try again,'' Abby said hopefully.

Madison shook her head. "I know when the evidence is stacked against me. He got that same look in his eyes that he always gets when he talks about you.''

Abby knew it was wrong to glow at the words. The hope bubbling up was a mistake. To even contemplate something with Nick was asking for heartbreak. But again she had to ask. "What look?''

Madison smiled sadly. "It's an expression that I hope some man someday will get when *my* name comes up.''

"What look?''

"It's hard to describe."

"What look?" she asked for the third time.

"As if you hung the moon." Madison sighed and shook her head.

"Really?" The question was rhetorical. She suddenly realized *why* she'd known Madison wasn't right for Nick. He'd never looked at her as if she held his heart in the palm of her hand.

"Despite what you've heard about attorneys, I always tell the truth. Yes, really." She moved toward the door. "One more thing. I like you, Abby. This would be so much easier if I didn't. Nick met you first. I never had a chance with him."

"Madison, I—"

She held up her hand. "Don't say anything. I think I'll go into the dining room and have a lovely glass of your very good house chardonnay."

Abby walked out with her. When they stopped at the bar, Luke was standing there.

"Great," Madison muttered. "Just what I need. Another Marchetti man."

Abby looked at the youngest Marchetti and thought Madison could do worse. He was very handsome. Not like Nick's charming, easygoing good looks, but with more of a simmering, dangerous appeal. In fact, as they stood in front of him, she looked from one to the other and thought they would make a striking couple—if Madison hadn't already been involved with Nick. No matter what she said, Abby hoped she would change her mind and be his significant other. She, Abby, wanted him to be happy. More than anything else in the world.

Luke smiled. "Hi, Maddie," he said.

"Hi, yourself," she answered.

"To what do we owe the honor of your presence?" Abby asked him.

Reluctantly, she thought, he pulled his eyes away from the other woman. "I was looking for Nick. I've left messages for him all day, and he hasn't returned them."

"I don't know why you thought he would be here," she said. "And before you ask, I don't know where he is. It's not my night to watch him."

Madison smiled a little sadly. "Before you ask, ditto for me."

Luke looked from one to the other. "Ma suggested I check here. I'll just catch him at the office tomorrow." He sat on one of the stools and met Abby's gaze. "I thought you might like to know that the restaurant numbers are up. Good job, Abby."

"That's great," she said. If only the rest of her life could be fixed as easily. "Thanks for letting me know, Luke."

"No problem." He turned his gaze to Madison. "You okay, Maddie? You look like you lost your best friend."

"No," Abby said quickly. "They're just taking a break."

"And you're the Queen of Denial," Madison said, smiling a little sadly.

"I have to get back to work." Impulsively, Abby hugged the other woman. "Thanks for trying to help."

As Abby walked away, she heard Luke ask, "Can I buy you a drink, Maddie? I have two shoulders. You can pick either one to cry on."

Abby closed and locked her car door. The wind was cold and her suit jacket was no protection. But it was the chill from inside that made her shiver. She hardly remembered the drive home from the restaurant. She was still reeling from Madison's revelation.

Nick never told her his secret.

That meant she, Abby, was the one he felt closest to. Was it possible that Madison and Sarah were right? Did Nick really have deep feelings for her?

Keys in hand, she walked through the apartment complex. As she approached hers, a man stepped from the shadows, startling her.

"Hi, Ab."

"Nick," she gasped, a hand to her chest. "You scared me out of a year's growth."

"Sorry. I didn't mean to. And you can't afford that. But I wanted to talk to you."

"You should have stopped by the restaurant. As a matter of fact, Luke was there. He was looking for you."

"I wanted to speak to you privately." He stuck his hands in his slacks' pockets, pushing up his suit coat. "I wanted to apologize for what happened with Sarah. You had a right to know what was going on with her."

"No, I'm sorry. I overreacted." She fumbled for her apartment key. "I'd been scared to death, and I took it out on you when all you tried to do was be supportive."

"You know what they say about hurting the ones you—"

"Darn it," she blurted out.

Her hand shook so badly, she couldn't get her key in the lock. Nick gently took it from her. Their fingers brushed, and for that fleeting moment, she savored the warmth of his skin on hers. She wanted to tell him to go away. She wanted to tell him to *never* go away. She wished she could curl up, pull the covers over her head and sleep for a hundred years with Nick beside her.

But that wasn't going to happen, so she might as well get this over with. They walked inside and she flipped on the lights, then closed the door. "Before you say anything, I've got a question for you," she said.

"Okay."

"Why didn't you ever tell Madison about Margaret?"

"How do you know I didn't?"

Abby set her purse on the table and took off her jacket. Then she turned to face him. "She came to see me at the restaurant tonight."

"She did?"

It was obvious Madison had told the truth. He hadn't put her up to it. Abby nodded. "Yes."

"Why?"

"She wanted to assure me that you two were not seeing each other anymore."

"How did the subject of Margaret come up?"

"I told her she couldn't hurt you like Margaret did. She didn't have a clue what I was talking about. What's up with that, Nick? Why did you tell me first? Before your family, and before the woman in your life?"

He rubbed a hand over his face. "It's so simple I didn't see it myself for a long time."

"I still don't see it."

"Yes you do, Abby."

The intensity in his gaze held hers. She wanted to look away and couldn't. She wanted to throw herself in his arms—and couldn't. Was it too much to ask that they just go on like always?

"Nick, don't say anything else. You're my boss. I don't want to compromise our work relationship."

His laugh was just this side of bitter. "We're way beyond that."

"No," she said, shaking her head. "We don't have to be. If we don't talk about this, it will just go away."

"That's fantasyland, Ab. It's not going away. At least not for me."

"I don't want to hurt you, Nick. I'm not right for you. I've got school to finish. So does Sarah. Then college. I have to work. I don't want a relationship until I have the time to see if it's right and make it work."

"When are you going to face what you're doing?"

"I face it every day."

He shook his head. "In a pig's eye. You're burying your head in the sand."

"That's what Madison said."

He smiled grimly. "You know what happens when you bury your head in the sand?"

"I have a feeling you're going to tell me."

He came close to her, so close that she could smell the lingering, sexy scent of his cologne. So close that she could see the pulse in his neck pounding. So near that she felt his warmth and security. With his knuckle, he nudged her chin up so she had to look him straight in the eye.

"I feel it's my duty as your self-appointed guardian angel. When you stick your head in the sand, you leave that very shapely rear end of yours exposed."

"How do you do that?" she asked. "Maneuvering Marchetti. How do you manage to insult me and dish out a compliment at the same time?"

His grin was fleeting. "It's a gift."

"I wish I had the gift. Because I can't give you what you're looking for, Nick."

"Yes, you can. I'm asking for a chance—for us."

"I don't have time."

He gripped her upper arms. "Hogwash. You've been hiding behind your responsibilities so long it's like a fortress. You're like the lonely princess in the ivory tower."

"This isn't a fairy tale. And you can't be my knight in shining armor."

"Yeah, I can. If you'll let me."

"I'd like to—if you still feel the same way a couple years from now."

"Why can't you have a life at the same time? You have a right to be happy."

"Do I?" she asked. Before he could answer, she said, "All I need is time. And your friendship. Just give me that, Nick."

"How about if I give you this instead?"

He lowered his mouth to hers. The kiss was surprisingly gentle for all the fierce anger she sensed in him. His lips were warm and soft, persistent and oh so persuasive. She felt a tightness in her breasts, and liquid heat that trickled through her and settled low in her belly and her most feminine place. She tried to stay aloof, but he deepened the kiss, urging her mouth open with his tongue. He slipped inside and she sagged against him.

He wrapped his arms around her and held her close. When he lifted his mouth from hers, his breath stirred the hair around her face. He whispered in her ear. "Abby, I—"

She pushed away from him. "I can't, Nick."

"You mean you won't." Hurt filled his eyes. "You're a coward."

"I'm not—"

"Whatever happened to the courageous young

woman I first met? The one who stood in my office and vowed to be the best employee I'd ever had? Because her parents had just died. Because she needed a job to support herself and her sister. That Abby was the bravest woman I've ever known. That Abby was the woman I fell—"

"Don't say it, Nick," she held up her hand. "Please don't say any more."

This was the second time in the last five minutes he'd tried to say the words. She couldn't let him. If she could prevent it, maybe she could avoid being his strike three. Most important, she could prevent any harm to his heart.

How she wanted to throw caution to the wind and go on the journey with this wonderful man. But her spontaneity had died in that accident with her parents. It had taught her that she couldn't afford to be reckless. Disaster was right around the corner. She had to protect herself as best she could.

"Abby, I—"

She held her hand up to stop him. "It's late. It's been a long day, and I still have to study for exams. I appreciate you stopping by, but I have stuff to do."

The old stuff-to-do excuse. It sure didn't diminish the pain she saw in his eyes. Gathering every ounce of her willpower, she forced herself to stand very still and not wrap her arms around him and tell him she was the worst kind of fool. And more important—she loved him and hoped he wouldn't hold her stupidity against her.

But all she did was watch him walk to the door and open it. The anger in his eyes made her flinch. "Strike three, Abby."

Then he walked out and slammed the door. Abby

refused to let the tears fall. The wonderful, special thing they'd shared was over. If only she could give him what he wanted. If only things hadn't gotten serious. And she had tried so hard not to let that happen. Because she'd been so sure that if she fell in love with him she would lose everything, including his friendship.

Being right hurt so very much more than she'd ever imagined.

Chapter Twelve

"For the record, you can stop matchmaking. Abby and I are kaput."

Nick had gone from Abby's place to his folks'. Now he sat at his mother's kitchen table and looked at the hot chocolate she'd set in front of him. He waited for her to say something. Her uncharacteristic silence puzzled him.

"Aren't you going to say something, Ma? You could at least do the token disclaimer about your efforts to get us together."

"Why? A mother can only do so much. Now it's up to you. How do you plan to win her back?"

"I just told you, she doesn't care about me. She told me to hit the road and don't come back."

"She didn't mean it."

"Yeah, Ma. She's been sending me these signals for weeks now. I've just been too dense to get the message."

"You're dense if you think that's the message she's been sending."

"What does that mean?"

Flo Marchetti pulled the belt of her flannel robe tighter and sat across from him. She dipped her tea bag in the steaming water in front of her. "It means that she's in love with you. Why do you think I kept the rest of the family from going to the cabin the weekend after Thanksgiving?"

"So you admit it."

"Of course." She nodded with satisfaction. "And I'm glad to see that for once they managed to keep their mouths shut. Rosie gave me the idea when she said she and Steve fell in love there."

"Thanks a lot, Ma. And remind me to thank my little sister, too. It was a disaster from beginning to end. In fact it was the beginning of the end. If I hadn't kissed her—"

"And?"

"And nothing. She backed off faster than you can say 'al dente.'"

Flo tapped her lip. "I wonder why. She's so in love with you. I saw it right away at Thanksgiving."

His laugh was bitter. "In *love?* Don't make me laugh. She doesn't have time. According to her, between work, school and Sarah—who's practically a grown woman, I might add—she doesn't have time to fall in love."

"She's afraid."

"She's the bravest woman I know," he said, leaping to Abby's defense. It didn't matter that only a short time ago he'd accused her of the same thing.

"Then she doesn't have the brains God gave an ant."

"Abby's one of the brightest individuals I've ever met. Look how far she's come since I first hired her. It takes keen intelligence to do that, with everything she's got going."

"You know, Nick, maybe it's for the best. She's really not all that attractive—"

"She's a knockout, Ma. Look, I just wanted to let you know what was going on. I don't have to sit here and listen to you bash the woman I love."

Flo smiled like the cat who ate the proverbial canary. "I knew it."

"So you were baiting me?" When she nodded, he said, "Don't look so smug. I knew it, too. But to respond to your earlier question of what I intend to do about it, the answer is nothing. Because you're wrong. Abby doesn't feel the same about me. She wouldn't even let me say the words. Every time I tried to tell her I love her, she stopped me."

"Poor Abby," Flo said, shaking her head sadly.

"What about me?" he asked. "My own mother! I'm your flesh and blood. You're supposed to take my side."

"I *am* your mother, and it was my fondest hope that none of my children would grow up to be a fool."

"Now just a minute, Ma. I don't think it's foolish to cut my losses and walk away when the woman obviously doesn't share my feelings."

Flo pointed at him. "That's where you're wrong. She loves you, or she wouldn't have stopped you from telling her. She's trying to spare you the same hurt that you got from that witch in Phoenix. You just have to figure out what's holding her back. She's proved that she's a stayer. She doesn't desert the people she loves. But she won't admit her feelings unless she's sure they're the forever-after kind. And remember, Nick, she's been through a terrible ordeal. She had firsthand experience that forever-after can be over in the blink of an eye.''

''Abby *has* been through a lot, Ma. But—''

''No buts. Fate took her parents from her and sent her world spinning out of control. By refusing to admit she loves you, she's grasping to hold on to her world. She's afraid of being hurt. If you run out on her, it will convince her that she's right to keep from getting close to anyone.''

Nick thought about what his mother said. He knew how it felt to have the props knocked out from under you. Not the way Abby had, but enough. Now he realized that he and Margaret were wrong from the beginning—a fire so hot it had quickly burned out, leaving nothing but ashes. What he had with Abby had grown over time to something pretty terrific. But he'd hibernated all these years because he didn't want to be hurt again. *Was* doing the same thing? And by clamming up, not wanting to hurt him again, she was showing him—not telling him—how she felt about him. That she did love him.

He couldn't give up and walk away. Without a doubt, he knew Abby was the one woman who could coax him from confirmed bachelorhood and give him everything he wanted in life. But he had to do what he'd been doing since he first met her, just keep showing up.

Abby wearily sat down on her love seat and rubbed her eyes. She was tired to the bone, but grateful that finals were over. It had been several days since she'd seen Nick. Coincidentally, it had been about that long since she'd slept. She couldn't forget the look on his face just before he slammed out the door. Every time she remembered, her heart cracked a little more.

If only she didn't love him so much.

He'd been right to try to tutor her in relationships. She was so backward. Recalling the kiss they'd shared in that romantic cabin, she sighed. And at the thought of the one in this very room, she groaned. His classes had been the best she'd ever taken. For all the good it had done. She would never take the final in that course. She'd managed to flunk out royally. Was it too late? Maybe there was a makeup exam, or an extra-credit assignment.

She had no experience in right or wrong for this situation. No frame of reference at all. But every instinct she had told her to go to him. Tell him how she felt. Beg him to forgive her. She didn't want to lose him completely. If he couldn't love her, she still wanted him in her life as a friend.

Sarah walked into the kitchen and poured herself a soda, then sat beside her on the couch. "Can I talk to you?"

"Of course."

"Nick told me I should apologize for my behavior and really mean it this time. I didn't think about worrying you the other night. He said I lied in a passive aggressive way, whatever that means."

Abby couldn't help smiling. That was Nick. Management double-talk. She squeezed her sister's hand. "It's okay, sweetie. He told me I have to lighten up on you so you'll be better prepared when it's time to fly this coop."

Sarah grinned. "That sounds like him. So we're okay?"

"You're all I've got in the world. You bet we are."

A frown creased her sister's smooth brow. "You've got Nick, too. Although he's been real down since the night of the winter formal. I told him you were taking finals. But he still doesn't sound like himself."

"It's okay. We talked." Abby could almost feel her heart breaking. But the last thing she wanted to do was cry in front of Sarah. "I guess he just finally got the message."

Sarah snapped her fingers. "That reminds me, I took a message for you before you got home from work." She jumped up and ran to her bedroom, then came back with a napkin in her hand. "It's from Luke."

What Abby read made her heart nearly stop and her blood run cold. Spots bounced before her eyes and she shook her head to clear it. She read it again.

"M & M Marchetti. Alex. Nick at the hospital."

She stared at Sarah. "What's going on? What does this mean?"

Her sister looked shaken. "I was on the phone with Austin when he beeped in. I was only half listening and jotted down a couple words. I'm so sorry, Abby."

"Nick's at the hospital?" Abby shook her head. "Oh, God. Not again. Not Nick."

She jumped up and grabbed her purse from the kitchen table. "I'm going to find him."

"Do you want me to go with you?" Sarah asked.

More than anything, Abby thought. Then she said, "Maybe you should stay here in case Luke calls back."

Biting the corner of her lip, Sarah nodded. Then Abby raced from the apartment to the carport. As she turned the key in the ignition, she prayed, "Please God, let him be all right. So I can tell him I love him."

* * *

Abby ran into the Regional Medical Center and stopped at the information desk. She wanted to scream at the operator to get off the phone and tell her where Nick was. But she held back. Barely.

Finally the woman looked up. "Can I help you?"

"Do you have a Mr. Marchetti here?"

The operator checked a computer screen and nodded. "Second floor. Room 208."

"How do I get there?" Abby asked. As frantic as she was, she was surprised that she'd made it to the hospital in one piece. Now that she was there, she didn't want to waste any more time trying to find him. Time, always her enemy, was still playing havoc with her life.

The woman pointed to her left. "The elevator is that way, on your right."

Abby nodded and ran down the hall to an empty elevator car. She punched the up button and in less than a minute was whisked to the second floor.

She exited the car and ran to the nurses' station. Before she could find someone to give her information, she spotted Flo and Tom Marchetti standing in the hall. Luke and Joe were there too, lounging against the wall. That must be where Nick was.

She hurried down the hall. Flo saw her coming and waved.

"How is he?" Abby asked. "I just got the message. Is Nick all right?"

"I'm fine."

Abby whirled around and saw him standing in the doorway to the room. He looked amazingly healthy, and annoyingly cheerful. Seeing him perfectly all right snapped the tension that had powered her. Stripped of all her defenses, she burst into tears. Covering her face with her hands, she turned away.

"Abby? What's wrong?"

That was Nick's voice. She felt his arms around her and without hesitation she pivoted to bury her face against his chest. "What's wrong, honey?" he asked again, his voice so gentle and kind she ached from the sweetness.

"The n-note said— You— Hospital." Abby tried to form words, but she couldn't stop crying.

"Let's find a quiet place," he said, leading her down the hall.

Abby was relieved when he didn't remove the arm he had around her. If this was the last time he ever spoke to her, she would remember this as the sweetest moment of her life.

By a row of windows, there was an informal waiting area. A couch and several chairs with tables here and there furnished the space. Nick sat down on the couch. She started to back away, and he grabbed her hand and tugged her onto his lap, wrapping her in his strong arms.

She started to cry harder. He was too sweet for words. She didn't deserve it.

"Go ahead and cry. Let it all out," he said. "I think you've needed this for a long time."

Abby didn't know how long she cried, or how long he held her while she did. Finally, feeling more exhausted than she ever had in her life, she sighed. Then she lifted her face and brushed the moisture from her cheeks as she met his concerned gaze.

"You okay?" he asked.

She nodded. "You?"

"I'd be a lot better if you would tell me what's wrong?"

Her heart pounded again. "You first. Sarah took a message, a very incomplete one. Something about your parents, Luke, you and the hospital. Is someone here?"

"Alex has food poisoning." He saw her shocked look. "He's going to be fine, just needs rest. His quest to find a chef to handle the frozen-food line has taken a detour."

She let out a long breath. "I thought you'd been in an accident. I thought it was happening to me again."

"Like your parents?" When she nodded, he said, "Tell me."

She sniffled and pulled a tissue from her pocket. "It's my fault that they died." She watched his face as the words sank in and before he could tell her how awful she was, she went on. "I wanted them to patch up the relationship. I didn't want to be the only kid in my circle of friends whose parents were divorced. I didn't want my life to change." She laughed bitterly. "They talked about going away for a long weekend to try to work things out. Then they decided against it because of leaving Sarah and me. I told them I was perfectly capable of looking after my little sister." She took in a shuddering breath. "My last words to them were a promise to take good care of her. I've been doing it ever since."

"You didn't kill them."

"If I hadn't insisted that I could watch Sarah, they would have stayed home. They would be here. They might not be together, but I could tell them how much I love them."

"Thanks for telling me, honey. It explains everything." He gave her a reassuring squeeze. "But it's not your fault they died. No one knows why terrible things happen. It's not good enough to just say it was their time. It's a lousy, stinking rotten thing.''

She nodded. ''And it's reminded me that life is precious, fragile and tenuous. We need to make every second count.''

''I couldn't agree more,'' he said. ''Which is why there's something I need to tell you.''

''There's something I need to say first. You were right, Nick. I have been hiding behind my responsibilities. It was hard losing my parents, then getting dumped by guys who were scared off by my situation. I couldn't compete, so I took myself out of the game. It was easier not to play than to fail. Or be hurt. But you changed all that.''

''Me?''

The corners of her mouth quirked up. ''You know good and well it's you. Not once did you give up on me. Except the other night. I've probably messed up any chance with you. God knows I don't deserve a second one. But I have to say this before I lose my nerve.'' She looked him straight in the eye and spoke from her heart. ''I love you, Nick.''

''Can I talk now?''

''Yes,'' she said, then held her breath.

''I love you, too.''

Abby bubbled with so much happiness, any second she expected to float away with it. She couldn't believe she'd heard him right. ''You love me? Even though I've been such an idiot?''

''As I so recently told my mother, you are the most intelligent, loyal, beautiful woman I know.''

''You talked to your mother? About me?''

He nodded. ''She made me see that a lasting relationship doesn't start with a flash fire. Mutual respect and admiration form a solid foundation to build love on."

"She's a wise woman."

"Amen to that. Especially when she told me to quit being a fool and go after you."

"She said that?"

"She understood that you were holding back because you were afraid of being hurt."

"Really?" Abby didn't know whether to be embarrassed, or run to his mother and kiss her. "I need to thank her," she said, starting to stand.

Nick held her firmly. "Not until I do this."

He took her face in his hands and touched his mouth to hers, gentle at first, but soon escalating to much more. This wasn't a tender kiss, but a passionate statement of their profound emotions, held too long in check. Abby absorbed the power of his love and put everything she had, all the force of her deep feelings into the meeting of their lips. She savored the moment when he wrapped her in his strong embrace, then put her arms around him, holding tight, as if she would never let him go.

It seemed like forever, but wasn't nearly long enough when they finally looked at each other. "Wow," he said, then dragged in air. He helped her up, then went down on one knee. "A more romantic setting would be nice, but we've wasted enough time already. I love you, and I'm not giving you a chance to change your mind or back out. Abby, will you marry me?"

"Yes," she said.

"Without regrets? Because it means you'll have to skip Footloose and Fancy-Free and go straight to Mar riage 101. Forever. Because I don't ever plan to let you go.''

"Promise?'' she asked fervently.

"Oh, yeah.'' His eyes took on an intensity she had never seen before. He stood up and took both of her hands in his. "I plan to spend the rest of our lives convincing you of something that's only just become clear to me. There could never be anyone but you. Madison knew it, and that's why she broke things off. She was right.''

"She's the best.''

He blinked. "You've really changed your tune.''

"I guess I've always been jealous of her. But it was very generous of her to come to see me and try to get us together.''

"Too bad it didn't help,'' he said wryly.

"Actually it did. Just not right away.'' She wrapped her arms around him and snuggled close. "But she planted the seed. What was she right about?''

"That I've been waiting for you since the first day we met. Somehow you sneaked into my heart, and it took me a long time to realize it.''

Footsteps sounded on the tile floor. "Well, isn't this sweet.''

Abby felt Nick turn. "Hey, Joe. You can be the first to congratulate us. We're getting married.''

"Another Marchetti bites the dust. I knew it.''

"What?'' Nick asked.

"That you two were just a matter of time. That day in my office, when I hugged Abby. You were jealous as hell.''

"So?'' Nick asked, not denying it.

"So I knew sooner or later you would bite the dust, leaving only three confirmed bachelors in the Marchetti family." Joe walked over to them and shook Nick's hand. He leaned over and kissed Abby's cheek. "Welcome to the family, Abby."

"Thank you," she said, loving the sound of that.

Nick put his arm around her shoulders. "You should try this, bro."

Joe shook his head. "Not me. No way I'm going down ball-and-chain lane. Not in a million years."

"You know what they say," Abby said. "Methinks he doth protest too much."

Nick grinned. "My future bride is right. Something tells me you're next." He smiled down at Abby then looked at his brother. "Just give in to it. You'll be glad you did."

"I certainly am," she said.

When Nick kissed her again, Abby was very glad he did. He went right from knight in shining armor to the Hero Hall of Fame. Just when she'd given up hope of a happy ending, he put the color back into her world. He was the kind of man who would be there forever. And then some.

*   *   *   *   *

Don't miss the next book in the Marchetti family saga. Joe's story will be coming only to Silhouette Romance in early 2000.

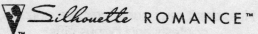

Looking For More Romance?

Visit Romance.net

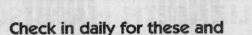

Look us up on-line at: http://www.romance.net

Check in daily for these and other exciting features:

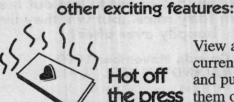

Hot off the press

View all current titles, and purchase them on-line.

What do the stars have in store for you?

Horoscope

Hot deals

Exclusive offers available only at Romance.net

Plus, don't miss our interactive quizzes, contests and bonus gifts.

PWEB

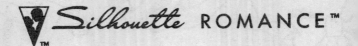

Silhouette ROMANCE™

Join *Silhouette Romance*
as more couples experience
the joy only babies
can bring!

Bundles of JOY

**September 1999
THE BABY BOND
by Lilian Darcy (SR #1390)**

Tom Callahan a daddy? Impossible! Yet that was before Julie Gregory showed up with the shocking news that she carried his child. Now the father-to-be knew marriage was the answer!

**October 1999
BABY, YOU'RE MINE
by Lindsay Longford (SR #1396)**

Marriage was the *last* thing on Murphy Jones's mind when he invited beautiful—and pregnant—Phoebe McAllister to stay with him. But then she and her newborn bundle filled his house with laughter...and had bachelor Murphy rethinking his no-strings lifestyle....

And in December 1999, popular author
MARIE FERRARELLA
brings you

THE BABY BENEATH THE MISTLETOE (SR #1408)

Available at your favorite retail outlet.

Silhouette®

Of all the unforgettable families created by
#1 *New York Times* bestselling author

NORA ROBERTS

the Donovans are the most extraordinary. For, along with
their irresistible appeal, they've inherited some rather
remarkable gifts from their Celtic ancestors.

Coming in November 1999

THE DONOVAN LEGACY

3 full-length novels in one special volume:

CAPTIVATED: Hardheaded skeptic Nash Kirkland has *always*
kept his feelings in check, until he falls under the bewitching
spell of mysterious Morgana Donovan.

ENTRANCED: Desperate to find a missing child, detective
Mary Ellen Sutherland dubiously enlists beguiling
Sebastian Donovan's aid and discovers his uncommon abilities
include a talent for seduction.

CHARMED: Enigmatic healer Anastasia Donovan would do
anything to save the life of handsome Boone Sawyer's
daughter, even if it means revealing her secret to the man
who'd stolen her heart.

Also in November 1999 from Silhouette Intimate Moments

ENCHANTED

Lovely, guileless Rowan Murray is drawn to darkly enigmatic
Liam Donovan with a power she's never imagined possible. But
before Liam can give Rowan his love, he must first reveal to
her his incredible secret.

Silhouette®

Available at your favorite retail outlet.

COMING NEXT MONTH

#1408 THE BABY BENEATH THE MISTLETOE—Marie Ferrarella
Bundles of Joy
Natural-born nurturer Michelle Rozanski wasn't about to let Tony Marino
face instant fatherhood alone. Even if Tony could be gruffer than a
hibernating bear, he'd made a place in his home—and heart—for an
abandoned child. And now if Michelle had her way, they'd *never* face
parenthood alone!

#1409 EXPECTING AT CHRISTMAS—Charlotte Maclay
When his butler was away, the *last* replacement millionaire Griffin Jones
expected was eight-months-pregnant Loretta Santana. Yet somehow she'd
charmed him into hiring her. And now this confirmed bachelor found
himself falling for Loretta...and her Christmas-baby-on-the-way....

#1410 EMMA AND THE EARL—Elizabeth Harbison
Cinderella Brides
She thought she'd outgrown dreams of happily-ever-after, yet when
American Emma Lawrence found herself a guest of Earl Brice Palliser's
lavish estate, he seemed her very own Prince Charming come to life. But
was there a place in Brice's noble heart for plain Emma?

#1411 A DIAMOND FOR KATE—Moyra Tarling
The moment devastatingly handsome Dr. Marshall Diamond entered the
hospital, nurse Kate Turner recognized him as the man she'd secretly loved
as a child. But could Kate convince him that the girl from his past was now
a woman he could trust...forever?

#1412 THE MAN, THE RING, THE WEDDING—Patricia Thayer
With These Rings
Tall, dark and *rich* John Rossi was cozying up to innocent Angelina Covelli
for one reason—revenge. But old family feuds weren't sweet enough to
keep the sexy CEO fixed on his goal. His mind—and heart—kept steering
him to Angelina...and rings...and weddings!

#1413 THE MILLIONAIRE'S PROPOSITION—Natalie Patrick
Waitress Becky Taylor was tempted to accept Clark Winstead's proposal. It
was an enticing offer—a handsome millionaire, a rich life, family. If only it
wasn't lacking a few elements...like a wedding...and love. Good thing
Becky was planning to do a little enticing of her own....

CMN1199